P9-AGI-622

"I want us to be husband and wife again, Carina."

Luis whispered the words, placing his hands around Carina's waist. "We were happy once, we can be again. I know it."

"My God, you've got a nerve!" Carina nearly shouted, as she knocked his hands away. "All those years of silence, and then we see each other for just a few days and you turn around and say you want me back. Has it ever occurred to you that I might not want you back?" she added venomously. "That I might like being free and independent?"

"And love?" Luis demanded tersely. "Can you live without that?"

"Love?" Carina laughed derisively. "All there is, is basic physical chemistry. It either lasts or it doesn't. And with us it didn't."

"No!" Luis grabbed her arm. "Stop being so defensive. Look into your own heart!"

SALLY WENTWORTH began her publishing career at a Fleet Street newspaper in London, where she thrived in the hectic atmosphere. After her marriage, she and her husband moved to rural Hertfordshire, where Sally had been raised. Although she worked for the publisher of a group of magazines, the day soon came when her own writing claimed her energy and time. Her romance novels are often set in fascinating foreign locales.

Books by Sally Wentworth

HARLEQUIN PRESENTS

HARLEQUIN ROMANCE

Don't miss any of our special offers. Write to us at the following address for information on our newest releases.

Harlequin Reader Service
901 Fuhrmann Blvd., P.O. Box 1397, Buffalo, NY 14240
Canadian address: P.O. Box 603,
Fort Erie, Ont. L2A 5X3

SALLY WENTWORTH

mistaken wedding

Harlequin Books

TORONTO • NEW YORK • LONDON
AMSTERDAM • PARIS • SYDNEY • HAMBURG
STOCKHOLM • ATHENS • TOKYO • MILAN

Harlequin Presents first edition January 1989
ISBN 0-373-11142-8

Original hardcover edition published in 1988
by Mills & Boon Limited

Copyright © 1988 By Sally Wentworth. All rights reserved.
Except for use in any review, the reproduction or utilization
of this work in whole or in part in any form by any electronic,
mechanical or other means, now known or hereafter invented,
including xerography, photocopying and recording,
or in any information storage or retrieval system, is forbidden without
the permission of the publisher, Harlequin Enterprises Limited,
225 Duncan Mill Road, Don Mills, Ontario, Canada M3B 3K9.

All the characters in this book have no existence outside the
imagination of the author and have no relation whatsoever to
anyone bearing the same name or names. They are not even
distantly inspired by any individual known or unknown to the
author, and all incidents are pure invention.

® are Trademarks registered in the United States Patent and
Trademark Office and in other countries.

Printed in U.S.A.

CHAPTER ONE

'BRITISH AIRWAYS regret to announce a further delay of approximately thirty minutes on Flight 432 to Lisbon, due to density of traffic.'

To Carina, the announcement was almost the last straw. If she hadn't been sitting in the Departure Lounge, with her luggage already checked in, she would have walked out of the airport and gone home again. And done so very gladly, because this was one trip that she was most reluctant to make. She had fought hard against going back to Portugal, with all its unhappy memories, but her mother had been more than obstinate, refusing to listen to any of Carina's arguments. In the end, she had lost the fight, not because of her mother's persuasiveness, but because Carina had been swamped by her own feelings of guilt and responsibility.

Giving up all attempts to read the glossy fashion magazine she'd bought for the journey, Carina picked up her bag and walked over to the noiseproof wall of windows that looked out over the busy airport. There was certainly a density of traffic; the big jets were coming in with only the briefest intervals between them, the morning sun reflecting off the bright colours of paintwork and logos, as they dropped out of the sky to land in unbelievable safety on the runway.

'I am not going to let history repeat itself. We've already had one broken marriage in this family because you were foolish enough to marry a foreigner, and I'm not going to let it happen to your sister, too.'

Her mother's determined words echoed in Carina's mind. Against them, all her protests and arguments had died, because there was no denying that her own marriage had been an abject failure. A holiday romance that had turned sour in less than a year.

'You must go to Portugal, find Stella and bring her back before she gets too involved with this man she's met,' Mrs Shelton insisted.

In angry reluctance, Carina had reached across the table to pick up the little pile of brightly coloured postcards, reading them for the third time.

'You see, she wrote about quite ordinary things, like the weather and the places she'd seen while she was in France, but when she got to Portugal she started mentioning this man that she'd met. Look, in this one she says that she's got a boyfriend and he's taking her to some city to see a castle. And in the next one, how much she likes him and that she's going to stay in Portugal for a while longer, instead of moving on to Spain. Then there are two more where she goes on about how wonderful he is. And now this last one.'

Carina looked at the card her mother was pointing to so forcefully, the one that had arrived only that morning. 'Have got a job in a bar,' her younger sister wrote in her sprawling hand. 'So I shall be staying here indefinitely. I'm so happy. It's so wonderful to be in love. I really think it's for keeps. I want to spend all my time with . . .' The next word was squeezed on the end of a line and was quite indecipherable.

'I can't make out the man's name,' Carina remarked. 'And she doesn't mention it in any of the other cards, just calls him her boyfriend. He may not be Portuguese,' she pointed out. 'He could be English.'

Her mother raised her eyebrows expressively. 'Whoever he is, it's still too fast. She hasn't had time to get to know him properly. He could be anybody, and yet here she is saying that she's staying in Portugal indefinitely. What's that supposed to mean? What about her place at university? Where is she?' She paused, her face white, then said deliberately, 'You know yourself that these so-called holiday romances don't last. You can't just sit by and let Stella make the same mistake you did, even if it does mean going back to Portugal. How could you live with your conscience if you let that happen?'

She was right, of course. Carina wouldn't wish that kind of heartache on anyone, let alone the sister she loved. Biting her lip, she looked again at the card, trying to make out the postmark. 'I think it was sent from Albufeira, which is about the biggest tourist resort there is on the Algarve. Even so, she might not be there—she could be staying anywhere along the coast.'

'Well, then, you'll have to use every means at your disposal to find her, won't you?' her mother said forcefully.

Raising her eyes, Carina looked unbelievingly into the older woman's set face. 'Do you know what you're saying?'

'Of course.'

'You're actually—encouraging me to see Luis again?'

'If asking for his help means that you'll find Stella more quickly, then, yes, I am.'

Getting agitatedly to her feet, Carina said, 'Mother, how can you possibly ask that of me? To see him again after all these years . . . it's impossible! I couldn't do it. I just can't believe that you'd ask it of me—especially after the way you've always persuaded me against seeing him or even answering his letters. How on earth can you expect me to just demand his help?'

'He's a lawyer,' Mrs Shelton pointed out. 'If he won't help you himself, he can at least put you in touch with someone who can. And while you're talking to him,' she added grimly, 'you can persuade him to apply for a divorce so that you'll be free of him at last.'

Carina bit back a sharp retort, knowing that telling her mother it was nothing to do with her would only make things worse. She had made the mistake of letting her mother interfere at the beginning, and there was no way now she could tell her to stay out.

The trouble was that until that fatal Spanish holiday Carina had been completely under her mother's domination. Her father had been killed in a car accident when she and Stella were young children and, instead of trying to make a new life for herself, Mrs Shelton had centred all her hopes on her children. She had always been an ambitious woman, although not for herself, only for her family; so, when she lost the chance to push her husband to the peak of his profession, she concentrated on her daughters' education, sending them to good schools and keeping Carina home to study instead of going out with her friends. Carina had always known that she must go on to university and take up a profession, that nothing less would do, and that only by doing so could she compensate her mother for all the sacrifices she had made. And in a strange way she felt that she also had to compensate for her father's untimely death, that her mother blamed him for the accident and only her daughters' success could take away the bitterness.

After taking her A-level exams, Carina had gone to Spain to improve her Spanish, her school having arranged for her to stay with a Spanish family. For the first time in her life Carina was on her own—but there she had met Luis and fallen instantly in love with his dashing good looks. Mrs Shelton, seeing a second set of hopes being ruined, had been furious when they had married, especially when Carina stayed in Portugal. If they had chosen to live in England she might have accepted the marriage, because then she could have been ambitious for both of them, but instead she wrote letter after letter, all urging Carina to come home. And when Carina finally did go back to give herself a break because the marriage wasn't working out, her mother persuaded her that if Luis really loved her he would stay in England with her. This Luis had angrily refused to do, with the result that they had parted in bitter fury.

By then it was too late for Carina to go to university, and she had had to live with her mother's recriminations and tears because Carina had failed her, until her sense of guilt was so heavy that she had had to move away, and had only then seen how self-centred her mother was: a selfish, embittered woman who was unable to accept that her children needed a life of their own. Yet, however much Carina tried to shake it off, the sense of guilt remained, and she knew that she must do everything she could to stop Stella making the same mistake she had.

'Will passengers for British Airways Flight number 432 to Lisbon please board at Gate number thirty-three.'

The announcer's voice brought Carina out of her reverie, and she turned to make her way towards the Departure Gate, walking with a cool elegance that drew many eyes to her tall, slim figure and shining fall of golden blonde hair. It was an outward manner that she had acquired over the last few years, this coolness, a guard that she had built up against people who wanted to get too close, ask too many questions. Especially men. Carina had been more than wary of men since that one tumultuous love affair with Luis that had led to a marriage that would never have taken place if either of them had been willing or able to listen to reason.

It was a business-class, scheduled flight, and Carina had a seat in the front, in the non-smoking section. The window seat was already taken by a man with hair so white-blonde that it could only have been bleached by constant exposure to the sun, a surmise proved correct by his deep tan. As Carina paused by the seat to take off the black straw boater that matched her crisp black and white suit, the man glanced up, his eyes widening with interest as he watched her. When she'd put her hat in the locker, he half rose. 'Would you prefer to sit by the window?'

Carina shook her head with a brief smile. 'No, thank you.' She sat down and clipped on her seat-belt, then sat back, her hands on the armrests, waiting for the take-off.

'Is this your first trip to Portugal?' the man next to her asked conversationally, his eyes openly admiring.

Turning her head to look at him, Carina registered that he seemed vaguely familiar, but she couldn't think why; she was sure she had never met him before. 'No, I used to live there.'

'Oh, really?' The man's eyebrows rose. 'That's interesting. I'm on my way to spend a few months there myself.' He paused, plainly expecting her to ask him why, but when she didn't, went on, 'Whereabouts did you live?'

'In Lisbon, mostly,' Carina answered reluctantly, remembering the tall grey house overlooking the park in the fashionable, lower area of the city. A house that Luis had taken her to after their marriage, and which they had had to share with his parents.

The plane began to taxi along the runway, and she gripped the armrests a little tighter, wishing that she could be as blasé about flying as the stewardesses who were demonstrating the life-jackets.

'Could you use a hand to hold?' her neighbour asked, smiling at her.

It was a warm, sympathetic smile, set in a handsome if rather rugged face, but Carina was in no mood to be receptive. Shaking her head, she said, 'Thanks, but I can manage on my own.'

The roar of the engines increased until it felt as if the plane was going to fall apart, and then hurtled down the runway to climb into the air in a perfect take-off. As soon as they levelled off, the stewardesses became busy with the drinks trolley and Carina relaxed, her knuckles going back to their normal colour. She bent to take the magazine from her bag, but the man next to her gave her no time to even open it before he said, 'Are you going to Portugal on holiday? To visit friends?'

'No, this isn't a holiday. It's—more of a business trip.' And there certainly wouldn't be any pleasure in it, Carina knew, her heart contracting at the thought of having to see Luis again after all this time. Especially since they had parted in such anger after the worst, most heated quarrel they had ever had. And that was saying something, because there had been a lot of rows and fights after those first few idyllic months of love and happiness. And there certainly wouldn't be any friends to visit—not being able to speak much Portuguese had almost completely restricted Carina's attempts to get to know Luis's friends or make any of her own.

'A business trip?' her neighbour was asking in surprise.

'Er—family business.'

'And is it likely to take up all of your time?'

Carina gave him more of her attention, recognising the opening gambit that could lead to an invitation—or a proposition. 'I really have no idea,' she answered coolly and opened her magazine, hoping he'd get the message and leave her alone.

'Would you like a drink?' The stewardess came along with the trolley and Carina ordered white wine, but the man next to her insisted on paying for it, despite her protests.

In the end, she had to accept the drink, and sat back with a rather stiff, 'Thank you.'

The stewardess gave him his change, smiled and said, 'Thank you, Mr Summers. I hope you enjoy your flight.'

Summers—the name, too, sounded familiar. A small frown between her brows, Carina said, 'I'm sorry, I'm sure we haven't met before and yet—well, you seem familiar.'

He gave her a lazy grin. 'Do you play golf?'

'Why, no.' She gave him a startled look.

'Then I doubt if we've ever met, but you might have read about me or something. I'm a golf pro. My name's Greg Summers.'

So *that* was how she'd heard of him, Carina realised: in the passing, casual way one does when one flips through the sports pages and glances at a photograph and headline, or turns on the TV set and finds a golf match in progress before one turns over to another programme. But if she, who had no interest in the game, had heard of him, then he must be quite famous.

'And are you going to Lisbon to play golf?' she asked, trying to remember if there was a golf course in the city, set—like Rome—among its seven hills.

Greg laughed, recognising that she didn't really know who he was, and not in the least disappointed. 'No, I'm meeting with some business partners who are financing a holiday development on the Algarve. I'll be in Lisbon to settle some legal matters for a week or so, and then I'm going down to the coast to superintend the layout of a new golf course at the holiday village.'

'That sounds quite a large undertaking.'

'Oh, it shouldn't take too long. It's mostly a matter of designing the layout to suit the land available. I expect to be able to play in quite a few tournaments while I'm over there.' They talked about the holiday village and time-share developments in general for a while, but then Greg gave her a lazy smile and said, 'I'm sure to have a few evenings free while I'm in Lisbon. Maybe we could get together and go out to dinner?'

'I'm afraid my plans are unsettled. I may not be in Lisbon for more than a couple of days, and then I'll probably be going down to the Algarve myself.'

'Really? What part?'

'I'm not sure. I may be travelling around.'

A meal that the stewardess described as brunch was brought to them on the usual plastic trays, but Carina hardly touched hers, although she drank the coffee gratefully. She couldn't help but dwell on the fact that every mile was taking her closer to Luis. Talking to Greg Summers helped to take her mind off it, and she asked him where the new golf course and holiday village was to be built.

'A few kilometres from Albufeira.' Then, seeing her surprise, asked, 'Do you know it?'

'Not really. It's just that—a relative of mine has been staying in Albufeira. At least, she sent a card from there.'

'And will you be looking her up?'

'I hope to,' Carina admitted feelingly, wondering if Stella was still in the area, and how long it would take to find her. As for persuading her to go home ... Carina pushed that problem aside. Sufficient unto the day—and today she would have to face Luis.

'Is anything the matter?' She turned to find Greg watching her keenly. 'You look rather pale.'

'No, I'm all right.' It was rather an effort, but she managed to smile back at him.

'You haven't told me *your* name,' he reminded her.

'It's Carina ...' She hesitated for a moment, wondering whether to use her maiden name, as she often did now, but something made her say firmly, 'Carina Riveiro.'

Greg looked at her with renewed interest. 'That doesn't sound very English. Could it be a Portuguese name?' he hazarded.

'Yes, it is. It's—it's my husband's name. He's Portuguese.'

'Oh, I'm sorry.' Greg drew back a little. 'You aren't wearing a ring,' he pointed out rather ruefully.

'No. I—actually my husband and I have lived apart for quite some time.'

'I see.' Greg relaxed again. 'And I suppose that's the—er—family business you've come here to deal with?'

'Partly,' Carina agreed, deciding that if he asked any

more personal questions she would immediately freeze him out.

But he seemed content with that and merely asked how long she expected to stay in Portugal.

'I've no idea. It depends entirely on how long it takes to—to do what I came for.'

The pilot's voice came over the intercom, telling the passengers that they were about to land at Lisbon airport, and warning them to do up their safety straps as they expected a little turbulence as they approached. Carina did up her belt and tried to relax. Greg said something to her, but she didn't hear him properly and turned to ask him to repeat it just as the plane hit an air pocket and seemed to drop about twenty feet through the sky. With a gasp of fright, Carina reached for the armrest, but the next second Greg put his hand out towards her and she gratefully grabbed hold, twining her fingers tightly in his as the plane buffeted for several minutes. It flew out of the turbulence at last, but Carina continued to hold Greg's hand until they landed and the seat-belt sign had gone out. Then she looked at him rather shame-facedly. 'I'm terribly sorry. I hope I didn't dig my nails in too hard?'

He gave her a woebegone look. 'I may never be able to play golf again.'

Carina laughed, enjoying being teased now that they were safe on the ground again. 'Well, thanks for the loan of your hand. I'm very grateful.'

'Any time,' he told her with a wide smile, and stayed beside her as they got off the plane and went into the airport to wait for the luggage to be unloaded. There he said, 'I suppose you'll be staying at a private house while you're here?'

'No.' Carina shook her head, looking more sophisticated now that she had replaced her hat. 'I'll stay at a hotel.'

'Which one?'

'I don't know yet. One somewhere near the outskirts of the city, I expect.'

'Is anyone meeting you?'

Her eyes grew shadowed, wondering if Luis would have come to meet her if she'd let him know that she was coming. But she hadn't wanted to run the risk of having him ignore her or refuse to see her. 'No, this is a—sort of surprise visit.'

Greg gave her a shrewd look. 'It sounds to me as if you might need some help while you're here. Look——' he took a notebook from his pocket and wrote on it, '—this is the name of my hotel. Promise me that you'll at least phone and let me know where you're staying, as soon as you get fixed up.'

Carina hesitated, not wanting to get involved. Greg was pleasant enough, and if she'd met him back home in London she would probably have enjoyed going out with him, but trying to find Stella and having to face Luis again would be traumatic enough without having anything else to cope with. She started to refuse. 'I really don't think . . .'

But Greg interrupted her. 'Hey, it's just in case you need a hand to hold again, OK?' Carina smiled, but obviously wasn't convinced so he added, 'There aren't any strings, Carina. I know that we've only just met and things may be pretty awkward for you just now. But you—well, you've made quite an impression on me. And I can't just let you walk away so that I never see you again. So please, say you'll phone and tell me where you are.' And he touched her arm, giving her one of his friendly, open smiles.

'All right.' Unable to resist his persuasiveness, Carina took the piece of paper and put it in her bag.

The carousel started to move as the first of the cases came through, and Greg put her suitcase on a trolley for her, then did the same with his own two large suitcases and a huge bag of golf-clubs.

Carina looked at it and raised her eyebrows. 'I wouldn't like to be your caddie.'

'Golfers mostly only use human caddies for big tournaments now. The rest of the time we use a golf buggy or else an electric trolley.'

While he was speaking they had walked out of the airport and over to the taxi-rank. He gave her case to the first driver and then turned to her, his eyebrows raised quizzically. 'Do you keep your promises, Carina?'

She laughed. 'I'll probably phone you within an hour. Goodbye.' She held out her hand and he shook it in a firm, warm grip. Then she turned and got into the taxi, waving to him as it pulled away.

'Where to, please?' the driver asked, and Carina found herself automatically answering him in Portuguese, telling him to go to a hotel near the Ministério da Justiça, near where Luis's office was situated. The first two hotels she tried were full, and she had to settle for a room in a smaller place, in a street leading into the town centre. She hadn't brought that many clothes with her, so it didn't take long to unpack and freshen up. Keeping her promise, she phoned Greg and gave him the name and number of her hotel, then quickly rang off before he could ask her for a date once more. Then there was nothing left to do except sit on the bed and gaze at the telephone, trying to find the courage to pick it up and phone Luis's office.

In the end, Carina told herself off for being a fool and picked up the phone, dialling the number that she still remembered off by heart. A woman's voice answered and Carina said, 'Could you tell me if Senhor Riveiro—Luis Riveiro, that is—is in his office today?'

'Why yes, he is, *senhora*, but he is at lunch at the moment and will not be back until two-thirty. Do you wish to make an appointment?'

'When will he be free?'

'I can make an appointment for you at three.'

'That will be fine. I'll call round then.'

'Your name, please, *senhora*?'

But Carina put the phone down, as much—she told herself—for Luis's benefit as her own; she could just imagine the flurry of gossip and anticipation that would run round his large office if they all knew that Luis's wife was coming to see him.

It was still only one-thirty, much too early to set out for her appointment, even if she walked the whole way, which she didn't feel like doing in the midday heat. She ought, Carina supposed, to have some lunch, but almost immediately dismissed the idea; her stomach was tied in too many knots of tension for her to be able to eat. But she also felt far too on edge to just sit in her hotel room and wait. In the end she took a taxi to Chiado, one of the main shopping centres of Lisbon, and walked to one of the quieter pedestrian ways, where café tables were set out under trees and big sun umbrellas. Here, Carina had a long, cool drink and watched the mixture of hurrying business people and ambling tourists, getting the feel of the city all over again. It was the sort of place to sit and linger, but she just couldn't relax, and as soon as she'd finished her drink went to look for another taxi.

As she passed a shoe shop, Carina glanced towards it and caught sight of her reflection in the large plate window. It was only a passing glance, but she registered how cool and sophisticated she looked in her stylish suit and the straw boater. The thought stayed with her when the taxi dropped her off at the tree-lined square opposite Luis's office building. Carina stood in the deep shade of a tree, looking across at it and remembering. She had been so young and inexperienced then, not in the least sophisticated, and vulnerable to every criticism from Luis's mother. To escape, she had often come to the office with Luis, to put letters in envelopes and stick on stamps, even occasionally being allowed to type letters to English clients. An occupation that had rapidly become unsatisfactory when she had eight ordinary and four advanced-level examination credits. She had even won a place at a good university, but she had gone on holiday to Spain before she settled down to working for a degree— and there she had met Luis, who was also on holiday.

Glancing at her watch, Carina saw that it was almost two-thirty, and her heart began to beat faster. Her eyes searched the road, and she saw that two men were walking along the pavement on the far side towards the office building, one of whom looked achingly familiar. Carina stepped back into deeper shadow, her chest so tight that it hurt and she could hardly breathe.

It had been so long that she had almost forgotten how tall he was. The Portuguese are not a tall race, but Luis was an exception, standing—at six feet and two inches— a good head taller than the man walking along beside him. He must have been to court that morning, for he still wore his black gown which flew loosely around him as he strode along, his companion having to almost run to keep up with his long strides. Carina smiled to herself, remembering how Luis had once said that she was the only woman he knew who could keep up with him. The boyishness was still in his step, although he was over thirty now, his youth left behind him. For a moment tears pricked Carina's eyes, but she hastily blinked them away, so that she could watch him again as he walked along in earnest conversation, often gesticulating with his free hand, his other carrying a heavy-looking briefcase. She had forgotten that, too—the way he gesticulated. Once she had loved it, because it was the most Latin thing about him, that and his fiery, unpredictable temper—and the way he made love.

A tight lump came into her throat and Carina had to turn away and lean against a tree trunk, her heart thumping. That side of their marriage had been so wonderful for the first few months, until other, outside influences, had ruined that, too. She closed her eyes tightly for a long moment and, by the time she'd recovered enough to look again, Luis was just entering the office building.

Slowly Carina made her way to a spare seat, biting her lip and realising that she couldn't face Luis feeling like this, not with all the old memories fresh in her mind. It was strange, she'd been sure that when she saw him again she would feel only bitterness and anger, the emotions she'd felt when they had last seen each other. But instead only the good memories had come flooding back, of closeness and love and discovery. Which was stupid, because they made her feel unsure of herself. Anger and bitterness she had long ago learnt to cope with, but she wasn't at all confident of handling softer emotions; she was definitely out of practice with these. Not that she'd ever been able to handle them particularly well, she thought morosely. She stirred restlessly, wondering whether it would be best to just cut and run, to go back to her hotel and try to find Stella without asking for Luis's help. After all, she hadn't given her name to his receptionist; he would never know that she had even come back to Portugal.

Getting to her feet, Carina took a couple of steps towards the road to look for a taxi, but then stopped, biting her lip as she looked up at the window of Luis's office. To run away would be the coward's way out, easy now, but something she would have to live with for the rest of her life. And surely she was old enough now to be able to control her own emotions. Suddenly the reflection of herself that she had seen in the shop window returned to her mind. Whatever she might be feeling inside, she certainly *looked* cool and composed enough. And it came to her that that was how she must play it. She must hide her feelings and be cold and aloof, act as if Luis mattered nothing to her now, that he had been only a youthful infatuation from which she had recovered long ago. Which, of course, was true. It was just having to see him again that had brought it all back. Yes, she must be impersonal and indifferent, merely an old acquaintance asking a favour of the only person likely to be able to help her. Carina's resolve shook for a moment as she remembered that last terrifying, blazing row before they'd parted for good. No, better not try and behave as if he was just an acquaintance, she decided, feeling nervous again. But she had almost twenty minutes before her appointment, and in that time she was able to think herself into the frame of mind she wanted, deliberately recalling some of the bad times to stiffen her resolve.

At exactly three o'clock, Carina walked across the road to Luis's office which took up the whole second floor of the building. Nervous tension, coupled with the determination to hide her feelings, made her look quite as cold and remote as she could possibly have hoped.

The receptionist looked up as she came in, but it was a new girl who gave her only a polite smile of enquiry. 'Can I help you?'

'Yes, I have an appointment to see Senhor Luis Riveiro. At three.'

'Oh yes, *senhora*, but you forgot to give your name.'

Carina swallowed and somehow managed to say calmly, 'I am Senhora Riveiro.'

The girl's eyes widened. 'You are a relation of Senhor Riveiro?'

'Yes. I'm ...' Her hands tightened. 'I'm his wife.'

She turned to sit down while the girl picked up the phone on her desk, vainly trying not to stare. As Carina sat down, a sudden thought flashed through her mind; what if, after all this time, Luis was living with another woman, someone he called his wife? Wow, that would really create a scandal in his father's austere law firm! But she knew instinctively that Luis would never do that, he would never live a lie.

'Senhor Riveiro won't keep you a moment,' the girl told Carina, eyeing her now in open curiosity.

'*Obrigada*,' Carina replied coolly, pulling her skirt down over her knees demurely.

A man, presumably Luis's previous client, came out of the door leading to the main offices, and the receptionist stood up. 'If you will come this way, please, *senhora*?'

Carina followed her and automatically stopped at the door of the office that had been Luis's, but the girl walked further on down the corridor, past the secretaries' big office to the one at the far end that had been the hallowed domain of his father, where he had seen only their most rich and respected clients, a room that she had never been into before. At any other time, she would have wondered about the change, but now all she could think of was seeing Luis again face to face, of having to speak to him after so long. Her heart began to jump crazily again, and she hesitated as the girl pushed open the heavy wooden door and waited for her to enter. Play it cool. Play it cool. The words repeated themselves in her numbed brain. With both hands tightly gripping her handbag, Carina took a deep breath and strode, tall and ice-cold, into her husband's office.

CHAPTER TWO

LUIS was standing over by the window with his back to her, looking down into the street. He waited until he heard the door shut, but even then it was a long moment before he slowly turned to face her.

He was the same, and yet so different. Although there had been youth in his step, there was no boyishness left now in his face. It was thinner than she remembered, with lines around his mouth that gave him a look of tight-lipped withdrawal, and the laughter in his long-lashed dark eyes had gone completely. But then, that had gone even before they had parted, and he was hardly likely to be amused at the moment.

Carina realised that he was looking her over just as closely and her chin came up. 'Hello, Luis,' she said coolly.

His brows flickered at her tone, but he betrayed no other emotion as he answered, speaking in English as she had done. 'Hello, Carina. This is quite a surprise.'

'Yes, I suppose it is. May I sit down?'

He indicated a chair with one of his eloquent gestures, then put his hand back in his pocket, as the other was. He didn't sit down himself, but remained standing, coming round to the other side of the big antique desk that had been his father's. His thick dark hair was shorter, he had worn it quite long before, but now he looked more conservative, older, and far more self-contained.

'I hope you don't mind me coming to see you in your

office,' Carina began. 'I thought it might be more private than if I'd called at the house.'

Luis's mouth twisted cynically, but he merely said, 'Not at all.' And waited for her to go on.

Seeing that he wasn't going to help her, Carina said stiffly, 'I hope your parents and the rest of your family are well?'

'As you have made absolutely no attempt to enquire after their welfare since you ran back to England, I can hardly think that it is of any real concern to you.' The words flashed out, sharp as a knife, betraying some of Luis's inner feelings.

Carina's eyes widened a little and went swiftly to his face, but it was as if he immediately regretted even that slight loss of control, because he said sneeringly, looking down his thin, aristocratic nose, 'I beg your pardon. It was, of course, merely a politeness, a form of speech.'

'I suppose so,' Carina admitted, not knowing quite how to go on.

There was a short, tense silence before Luis said, 'I suppose you must have had some reason for coming here. Or is it merely a social call, looking up old—aequaintances while you're in the city?'

His sarcasm helped, strangely enough; it made Carina's back stiffen and her voice become even colder. 'Yes, I have a reason. As a matter of fact, I came here to ask for your help, in—in a family matter. But I shall, of course, quite understand if you refuse. I know that I have absolutely no claims on your time or—co-operation.'

Luis looked at her for a moment, then turned and strode to the window again. 'But you are still my wife,' he pointed out, not looking at her.

'I wrote and offered you a divorce a long time ago.'

'So you did.' He turned to face her, his features a set mask.

'Don't you want your freedom?' Carina asked curiously.

'Do you want yours?' Luis countered. 'Is that why you've come here—to ask for a divorce?'

Slowly she shook her head. 'No, but if you want one ... I'm not sure about the law on divorce here in Portugal, but I think that in English law we've lived apart long enough for it just to be a formality if we both consent.'

'Perhaps, but we were married here, and there is also—the religious side to consider.' Abruptly, he changed the subject, taking his hands out of his pockets and putting them on the desk, leaning towards her. 'So, if it's not for a divorce, then why have you come?'

After hesitating a moment, Carina answered reluctantly, 'It's about Stella. My sister, you remember?'

'Yes, I remember.'

'Well, we're very worried about her. She took her A-levels this year and then decided to take a really long holiday before going to university, perhaps even taking a year's sabbatical. She went to France first, and was working her way through Europe. We didn't hear from her for quite a while, then we received a card from the Algarve saying that she was working in a bar—and that she'd met a man.'

At once, a gleam of amusement came into Luis's eyes. 'And your mother was, of course, terrified that she would have yet another daughter ruining her life by marrying a "nasty little foreigner".'

Carina went white, remembering how her mother had

actually been so angry that she had once described Luis in those words. 'I think it would be better if we left our respective parents out of this,' she said acidly.

'Oh, I quite agree.' Luis stepped back and looked down at her derisively. 'It would have been better if we had kept them out of our lives right from the beginning.'

Carina agreed with that sentiment whole-heartedly—especially with regard to *his* parents—but she held her tongue, not wanting to get involved in another fight at this of all times.

His lips twisting in wry amusement, Luis said, 'I see that you've learnt to control your temper a little?'

'And you yours,' she returned calmly. 'Well, will you give me your help to look for Stella or not?'

'What exactly do you want me to do?'

'To use your influence and knowledge to try and trace her. Presumably someone, some authority, has records of all foreigners entering the country. She might even have had to take out a work permit if she's working in a bar. But I don't know where to go, who to see. As a lawyer, it would be so much easier for you, save me such a lot of time.'

Crossing to the swivel chair on the other side of the desk, Luis sat down and leaned back, apparently completely at ease again, his fingers tapering together in a long pyramid. 'And just why do you think I should go to the trouble of helping you?'

It was strange, it hadn't even occurred to her before that he might not help her; she had just taken it for granted that he would. 'Out of common politeness, I suppose,' she answered with a shrug. 'I presumed that your family still have the villa in the Algarve and that you therefore still have contacts there. If you haven't ...'

'Oh yes, we still have the villa.' He paused for a moment. 'And supposing I do agree to help you—what do I get in return?'

Carina's head came up sharply. This was a mood she'd never seen him in before; he had never been devious, but now she could read nothing behind his enigmatic, almost cynical expression.

'Our gratitude, I suppose.' She gave a thin smile. 'I've already offered you the only thing I thought you could possibly want.'

He let that go with only a slight tightening of his jaw and said, 'And if Stella is still in Portugal, and you find her, what then? Will you make her go back to England with you?'

'That's the general idea,' Carina agreed.

'What if she refuses? What if she wants to stay with this man she's met?'

'Then I shall have to try and persuade her to give him up.'

Luis gave a short, harsh laugh. 'You hardly seem to be the right person to do that.'

'On the contrary,' Carina flashed back, 'I'm exactly the right person, because I've already learnt by my own mistake.'

Suddenly there was tension in the room again, like a living, breathing thing. Luis's face had hardened, his jaw thrust forward. 'You never gave it a chance to be anything but a mistake.'

A sharp retort came to Carina's lips, but somehow she managed to stifle it and stood up. Coldly, she said, 'I'm quite willing to admit that any mistakes in the past were mine, and I've obviously made another in coming here today. I'll find Stella on my own. Goodbye.' And she turned to walk to the door without a backward glance.

But as she reached it and put her hand on the knob, Luis said deliberately, 'I already know where Stella is.'

Carina turned to stare at him. 'But how could you possibly . . .?'

He gave an ironical smile. 'Despite my unpopularity with the other members of your family, I always got on very well with Stella. Probably because she was too young to be prejudiced against foreigners. We've always kept in touch. And it was quite natural for her to look me up and spend a few days here when she came to Portugal.'

Walking slowly back to the desk, Carina said, 'What do you mean, you kept in touch?'

'We exchanged letters occasionally.'

'You couldn't have done! Mummy would have noticed if Stella had letters with a Portuguese stamp.'

'I'm sure she would, if she continues to watch you both so closely, but I wrote to Stella through a schoolfriend. Oh, don't look so affronted, it was only a couple of times a year—at Christmas and on her birthday.'

'And what did you find to write about to a child over ten years younger than you?' A sudden sharp fear came to her—suppose Luis was the man Stella had fallen for? Her horror must have shown on her face. 'Good God, you're not the man, are you?'

Luis laughed in real amusement. 'Of course not! Even *I* wouldn't be foolish enough to let that happen. Not again. No, we mostly wrote about you—at first,' he said, his mouth growing grim.

Carina expected him to go on, wanted him to, but when he didn't she said tartly, 'And I suppose you encouraged her to come here? Where is she—at the villa?'

'She stayed there for a time, I believe, but she may have moved on. I gave her the freedom of the house for as long as she wanted it, but I haven't been keeping track of her movements. I'm not her guardian—just a friend,' he said meaningfully.

'And didn't your parents have anything to say about that? I can hardly think they would approve of another member of my family encroaching on their—hospitality, using their villa.' She would have liked to add that they had resented her, their own daughter-in-law, using it, but was in control of herself enough to refrain.

'My mother has been ill for some time, and is not in a fit state to care. I haven't even mentioned Stella's name to her.'

'Very wise,' Carina said drily.

Luis threw her a malevolent look. 'Anyway, who does or does not stay at the villa no longer concerns her. It belongs to me now.'

'To you?' She frowned. 'You've bought it from your father?' She paused, looking round her at the big office. 'And you've moved into his room?'

'My father died not long after you ran away to England,' Luis said heavily, confirming the surmise that had already come into her mind.

'Oh, but you should have told . . ,' Her voice trailed off.

Luis nodded and said harshly, 'Exactly. What would have been the point? You had made it quite clear—you and your mother—that you no longer wanted anything to do with me or my family.'

'That was a long time ago,' Carina cut in sharply. 'Circumstances have changed. I'm very sorry that your father died and your mother is ill.'

He looked at her, his lower lip, the full sexy one that she had loved to bite, pushing forward moodily. 'Thank you,' he said at length. 'Does that mean that you're no longer under your mother's influence?'

'I don't live at home any more, if that's what you mean. I have a flat of my own. But presumably you know that, if you've been writing to Stella.' The words 'behind my back' weren't said, but she certainly implied them.

'Whose idea was it to come here and find Stella?' Luis demanded. 'Yours or your mother's?'

'My mother's,' Carina admitted, but added quickly, 'But I was worried about her too. I didn't want her to go through—what I went through.'

His eyebrows rose scornfully, but Luis merely said, 'I will phone the villa this evening, and see if Stella is still there and let you know tomorrow morning.'

'Good, and I'll go down tomorrow afternoon.'

'No, you won't. Not unless she agrees.'

'Of course she'll agree. Why shouldn't she?'

'Maybe she won't want anyone interfering in her love affair. After all, you didn't, did you? For the first time in your life, you wouldn't even listen to your own mother.'

Twin splashes of colour came to cheeks grown suddenly pale as Carina retorted, 'If I had, we would both have been saved a great deal of—of unpleasantness.'

His mouth twisting wryly, Luis repeated, 'Unpleasantness! How you English understate things.' His dark eyes suddenly grew intense. 'But we would also have

missed a great many *pleasant* things besides. Wouldn't
we?'

Carina stood up, still outwardly calm and composed,
although her emotions were in rags. With icy politeness
she said, 'I'm staying at an hotel in the Rua do Salitre,
near the Botanical Gardens. Here's the telephone
number.' Taking a card from her bag, she put it on the
desk, ignoring his outstretched hand. 'Perhaps after
you've spoken to Stella you would be good enough to let
me know?'

'Still running away from situations you can't handle,
I see,' Luis remarked disparagingly.

Her chin coming up, Carina answered cuttingly, 'On
the contrary, there are some situations which are just too
boring for me to be interested in. Goodbye, Luis. Thank
you for your time. I do hope I haven't kept you from one
of your terribly important clients, but you can always
send me the bill for your—services.'

This time, Carina made it out into the corridor,
although she was more than half afraid that Luis would
lose his temper at that last gibe and come after her. She
noticed that several people just happened to be in or near
the corridor and her head came up. Let them look, let
them satisfy their curiosity. She could just imagine the
gossip and speculation that was already flying round the
firm. So, head high, Carina walked proudly down the
corridor and left with only a brief nod for the
receptionist.

It wasn't until Carina had crossed the road and made
it to the park again that reaction set in, and she had to sit
down hurriedly. Her heart was racing and her legs felt as
weak as if she'd been taking part in a twenty-six mile
marathon! Her emotions were a crazy jumble; relief that

this first meeting was over, anger at his arrogant assumption that everything that had gone wrong between them in the past had been her fault, and the heart-stopping attraction she'd felt from the first moment they'd met. The latter Carina was able to push to the back of her mind; she had fallen for that before and it had turned out to be only sexual—if 'only' was a word that could ever describe such life-shatteringly feverish desire. She was angry, too, that he had been writing to Stella behind her back. Heaven knew what her sister had told him; Carina thought of one or two of the men she'd dated about a year after she'd left Luis, when the deep ache of loneliness had become unbearable, and shuddered at the thought of Stella describing the relationships to him. When she finally got hold of Stella she was going to have a very sisterly word with her about that! *When* she got hold of her . . .

Getting to her feet, Carina began to stroll through the little park, and then along the busy streets. It wasn't so hot now and walking was bearable, but her thoughts were hardly on her surroundings at all. Although she tried to keep her mind on other things, she couldn't help thinking about Luis, about how much he'd changed, seeming so much more mature now. Had responsibility done that to him? Having to take over his father's law firm before he was thirty must have been quite a headache, but he appeared to be coping—the office still seemed as busy, anyway. And he'd said that his mother had been ill for some time, so as he was her only child that, too, must be quite a responsibility. Fleetingly, Carina wondered if his mother was still so possessive of him, refusing to give him up even to his wife. When they had first been married, Carina had been willing enough

to share him, knowing that he meant everything to his
parents, but she had soon been forced to realise that his
mother had no intention of sharing him; she wanted
Luis back and was determined to get him. And she had
won, quite easily. Against the older woman's subtle,
undermining influence, Carina's youth and innocence
hadn't stood a chance. Not that Luis had been a mere
pawn between them, she had to admit that. But he had
been busy with an important lawsuit his father—
purposely, in Carina's opinion—had given him almost
immediately after their marriage. He hadn't seen the
difficulties she was going through, and her pride had
prevented her from telling him. He had expected her to
behave like a Portuguese girl and take a daughter's place
in his parents' household, learning from his mother's
guidance and instruction. However, helping her to
become a part of the family had been the last thing his
mother had intended. Carina smiled grimly to herself;
how galling, then, for his mother to have got rid of her
unwanted daughter-in-law so quickly, only to find that
no divorce and new marriage had been forthcoming.

Angrily, Carina pushed the thoughts of the older
woman from her mind. It had all been so long ago; what
could it possibly matter now? She felt thirsty, and
stopped at another café where she had a drink and a
selection of the small, appetising savouries that all the
cafés in Lisbon did so well. Forcing her mind back to the
present problem, Carina wondered whether Luis *would*
phone her about Stella. She much resented the high-
handed way he'd said that he would actually ask Stella's
permission first, and wondered if he was just being
bloody-minded. But immediately she dismissed the
thought; other men in the same position might stoop to

that kind of thing, but Luis had never been spiteful in
the past. Arrogant, impatient, short-tempered, yes, but
never malevolent. Should she not wait for his phone call,
but go straight down to the villa herself? Carina
wondered. His servants could hardly refuse her entry
when her sister was already there. *If* she was there; or if
she stayed there after Luis had warned her that Carina
was on her way to take her home. It was certainly a
problem, but in the end Carina decided to give Luis
until lunch time tomorrow. If he hadn't rung by then,
she would hire a car and go down to the villa, whether he
liked it or not.

The streets were crowded now with business people
making their traffic-jammed way home. There seemed
little point in trying to take a taxi or one of the
articulated trams, so she walked back to her hotel,
intending to bathe and change, find somewhere quick
for a meal, and then have an early night.

It was strange, she had only lived in the city for a
relatively short time, and hadn't been back for years, but
the sense of direction came immediately back to her and
she was able to make her way unerringly to her hotel,
without having to consult one of the maps of the city put
up for the convenience of tourists, or to ask the way.
When she reached it, the receptionist handed her a
message along with her key. Carina's hopes rose for a
moment, thinking it was from Luis, but when she
opened the note she saw it was from Greg Summers.
'I've been invited to a party tonight by one of my
Portuguese partners,' she read. 'If you're free, how
about coming along? I could certainly use an interpreter, and one as stylish as you would be a great boost
for my morale.' The message was signed, 'Greg' and

handwritten, so he must have callled at the hotel and left it for her.

Carina pondered over the note for several minutes. There were advantages and disadvantages to accepting it. On the one hand, she didn't want Greg to think that she was an easy pick-up and get the wrong idea about her, but she *was* at a loose end tonight, with nothing to do but perhaps take a walk after her meal—which wasn't always a wise thing to do when you were a woman alone in a big city. And, now that she'd seen him again, when she was alone she found herself thinking of Luis all the time, which she definitely didn't want to do. On this thought, Carina picked up the phone and rang Greg's hotel.

'Thanks for the invitation,' she said when he'd answered.

'Can you make it, or are you tied up with your family?'

Without committing herself, Carina asked, 'What sort of party is it?'

'Quite formal, I think. Certainly not wild, if that's what you're afraid of. Oh—and there aren't any strings either, if you're afraid of that, too,' Greg replied, with a note of laughter in his voice.

Carina smiled in response and said, 'Then I'd like to come with you.'

'That's great. I'll pick you up at eight.'

Luckily, Carina had brought a couple of evening dresses with her, although she hadn't really expected to need them. She chose a soft lavender-coloured dress with thin sequinned shoulder-straps, then washed her hair, blow-drying it into what she called her number three, semi-formal style, taking it back off her face, but leaving it loose at the back so that it brushed against her bare skin. Careful make-up, a pair of high-heeled shoes in a darker shade of lavender, her little silver evening bag with enough *escudos* to take a taxi back to the hotel if she needed it, and she was ready. Ready for quite what, Carina didn't know. The evening was an entirely unknown quantity, a date with a man she'd only just met, in a place she'd never been to before, and a houseful of strangers, and Portuguese strangers at that. A fleeting worry, that there might be someone at the party that she knew from the past, crossed Carina's mind, but such a chance was extremely unlikely; she had only lived here a few months and had met very few people, not getting to know any of them very well.

Greg called for her on time, looking very dashing in a white tuxedo. 'You look beautiful,' he told her. 'Thanks for coming along.'

'Where is the party?' Carina asked as they got into the waiting taxi.

'It's a house on the Rua João Nascemento da Costa.' Greg read from a slip of paper in his hand and made a terrible mess of the pronunciation. 'Do you recognise that mouthful?'

Carina laughed and shook her head. 'The Portuguese have a habit of naming their roads after national heroes, and they always use the whole name, instead of shortening it to Nelson Road or Wordsworth Drive as we do in England.'

'How did you get on this afternoon?' Greg asked. 'Have any luck sorting out your problems?'

'I'm not sure yet. How about you? Did your meeting go OK?'

'Well enough. But it's early days yet, and everyone's

being very polite to each other. I expect they'll be having a few arguments over money later on, but I want to build one of the best golf courses in the country, and that costs.'

'Do you think you'll get what you want?'

'Oh, yes,' he answered confidently. 'I just hope I don't get too much hassle along the way, that's all.'

Carina looked at him in some curiosity, realising that he was obviously a successful businessman as well as a golf pro. He had an air about him of easy affluence, his clothes were well cut, his shoes handmade, and there was also a gold watch on his wrist. Nothing flashy, just the casual self-confidence that came from not having to worry about where the next meal was coming from. Luis had it, too, but there was nothing at all casual about Luis.

The house where the party was being held turned out to be about twenty minutes' drive from the town centre, up in the hills to the east of the city. They were welcomed by one of Greg's partners, Antonio Alvor and his wife, a youngish middle-aged couple. They both looked at Carina with some interest when Greg introduced her and she spoke to them in Portuguese.

'Your accent is very good,' Senhor Alvor complimented her. 'But you are not, I think, Portuguese?'

'No,' Carina admitted. 'but I have—links with the country.'

Their host laughed. 'I thought not. We don't have many blondes in this country. Not natural ones, anyway.'

They all laughed politely at his joke, then he led them into the main room, where there were already several other guests gathered, and dutifully introduced them to everyone there. Among the guests were Greg's other partners, who spoke some English, but Carina found that she was quite often able to help out by translating for him. The party had been given in Greg's honour and he was much in demand, so she stayed by his side as he met and talked to other guests who arrived after them. They were introduced to one couple, both of whom looked at her intently when they heard her name, and for a moment Carina's heart sank, but she was almost sure that she'd never met them before and decided that they must just be curious about her being with Greg.

It was an hour before the food was served, and by that time Carina was ravenous. 'Don't think that I'm always this much of a pig,' she remarked to Greg as she filled her plate at the buffet table. 'It's just that I've had hardly a thing to eat today.'

'Didn't you have lunch?'

'No. I had time but I—but I couldn't eat.'

Greg shot her a glance. 'Your problems too much on your mind, I suppose?'

She nodded, grateful that he was so acute. They moved aside and found a couple of chairs in a corner. 'Would you like to tell me about it?' Greg asked. 'Or is it something you'd rather not talk about?'

Carina gave a small shrug. 'Oh, it's just the age-old story, really. I was too young to realise that what I felt was only infatuation and not love. We married, but it didn't work out.'

'And your husband? Was he too young as well?'

A shadow darkened Carina's eyes. 'He was twenty-eight.'

'Old enough, then, I should have thought,' Greg commented. He looked at her troubled face for a

moment and briskly changed the subject. 'You obviously speak Portuguese very well. Did you live here very
long?'

'No, only a few months, but I had a lot of lessons while
I was here, and when I went back to England—well, it
seemed a shame to just let it lapse, so I went to a language
school; one of those laboratory-type places where you
just hear and speak your chosen language all day long for
weeks. When I finished there, I managed to earn a living
as a freelance translator. Luckily for me, there aren't
that many people in my home town who can speak
Portuguese, so I was quite in demand.'

'And do you still do that?'

'More or less, but about a year ago I set up a
translation and secretarial agency, so I do more
administrative work now.'

They talked on while they ate, afterwards getting up
to mingle with the other guests again. Although Greg
was sociable towards everyone, he made it plain that he
was more interested in Carina, giving her his whole
attention whenever she spoke, asking her questions and
encouraging her to talk about herself. Which was all very
flattering and very good for Carina's ego. Having met
Luis again had made her ego feel a little tender today—it
could do with a boost.

She liked Greg, she decided; he was fun to be with and
had an easy, natural charm that seemed to draw
everyone to him. But then, he was a celebrity in his own
field and could probably have acquired the social charm
as he had become more successful. Carina began to really
relax and enjoy herself. It was pleasant to be able to
practise her Portuguese among the natives, the food had
been good, and there was plenty of *vinho verde* to drink.

She was being paid a lot of attention, not only by Greg, but also by the other guests, because they found it unusual to meet someone so fluent in their language, and because she was with the guest of honour, Carina supposed.

They had been at the party for over two hours when Carina heard their hosts greeting a newcomer and glanced over towards the door. The late guest had his back to her, but she only had to see the height of the man and the set of his shoulders for the party to immediately go sour on her. It could be no one else except Luis; no other man was that dark and tall, and had that arrogant way of holding himself.

For a moment, blind panic set in and Carina just wanted to turn and run before he saw her. Greg had gone to look at a very old map on the wall with one of his business partners, leaving her with just the partner's wife and son. She said a hurried, 'Excuse me,' to them and looked around for another way out of the room, but Luis and the Alvors were blocking the only exit. Quickly, Carina walked over to Greg and put a hand on his arm. He glanced at her, smiled, and covered her hand with his, but had to wait until the man with him had finished explaining some point on the map before he could give her his full attention.

In those few moments, Carina managed to stifle the panic and realise that she couldn't just run away. She would just have to face Luis, as she had this morning. But she cursed the malevolent fate that had brought them both to the same party. And she was here with Greg! Luis would be bound to think that she was in Portugal with him, unless he found out that they'd only met that day. Oh God, no, that was worse—then Luis would think that she was cheap and easy. Her mind whirling, and already feeling as if Luis's eyes were knifing into her back, Carina tugged at Greg's sleeve.

Seeing her anxious face, he quickly excused himself and turned towards her. 'What is it?'

'I'm—I'm afraid I'm going to have to ask you to—to do something for me.'

Greg's eyebrows shot up 'Huh?'

She drew him to one side. 'I don't know how it could possibly have happened—I don't know anyone here—but—but my husband has arrived.'

'He has? Where?'

'No, don't look round! Look, before he talks to us, I want to ask you a favour. Would you *please* say that we've known each other for some time? I don't want him to know that you—that we only met this morning.' She spoke urgently, her hand gripping his sleeve.

'OK, if that's what you want. Does he know you're here? Who could have told him?'

'I've no idea. But I'd like to leave as soon as possible, please.'

'All right. But in the meantime, why don't we have another drink?' Putting his hand casually round her waist, Greg led her over to the bar and refilled her glass with wine. He smiled at her. 'Don't look so worried. I'm not going to let him hurt you. If he starts to make a scene, I promise to have you out of here within two minutes.'

Seeing the confidence in his eyes, Carina began to relax a little and sipped her wine. What he'd said was true; Luis would never make a scene in a public place, so there was really nothing to be afraid of. So why was her heart thumping and her pulse racing so fast? Carina wondered bleakly.

She was standing with her back to the room and only half listening to Greg, her ears pricked for the sound of Luis's voice behind her. As Greg talked lightly, his eyes went over her shoulder, watching the room. Carina saw them widen a little, although his voice hardly faltered, and she knew that Luis was coming up to them. She steeled herself to meet him, to be as cold and detached as she had been this morning, but her fingers were holding her glass very tightly, and she would have given almost anything to get away from there. She began to talk very animatedly to Greg, and they were both laughing when Luis's voice, very dry and cold, came from behind her.

'Good evening, Carina.'

Carina turned to face him and managed to simulate astonishment quite credibly. 'Why, Luis! What a surpise. Have you been here long? I'm afraid I didn't notice you before.'

'No, not long.' He held a glass in his right hand, the other was thrust into the pocket of his dark evening-suit. His eyes went over her head, but it was impossible to read his feelings. Then his eyes moved to Greg.

'This is Greg Summers, the—er—guest of honour. And this is Luis Riveiro,' she introduced them.

'How do you do?' Luis responded, but made no attempt to shake hands. 'I understand that you're in partnership with Antonio Alvor on his Algarve development venture?'

'That's right,' Greg agreed. 'Is that your line of business, too?'

Luis smiled thinly. 'Not quite. I'm a lawyer. I represent one of your partners.' And he gestured across the room to the man and woman who had looked at Carina so intently earlier. The couple were watching them now, but quickly turned away when they realised Luis was talking about them.

The suspicion immediately crossed Carina's mind that they must have telephoned Luis and told him that she was there as soon as they had heard her name and realised who she was. Frowning, she lifted her head to ask him, but didn't even have to say a word; the gleam of amused irony in Luis's dark, expressive eyes told her that she had guessed correctly. Angry indignation filled her and Carina gave him a disdainful look. 'You have spies everywhere, it seems.'

Luis's expression hardened. 'It appears that I might need them.' And he looked at Greg significantly.

Carina felt like telling him that it was none of his damn business, but Greg said quickly to Luis, 'Then I suppose I'll be seeing you tomorrow, when we all meet to settle the legal details of the partnership?'

Luis nodded. 'Yes, I shall be there.' He glanced at Carina. 'Quite a coincidence, you knowing my wife.'

If he had intended to surprise or disconcert Greg, he didn't succeed. 'Yes,' Greg agreed. 'Isn't it?'

'Have you known each other long?'

'Quite some time.' Greg smiled at Carina and put his arm round her waist, drawing her to him. 'How long is it now, darling? About six months, I think.'

Carina's heart went into her mouth—she tried to hold herself away from Greg, but he wouldn't let her. Lifting her head, she looked at Luis to see how he was taking it, and was stunned by the blazing anger that flashed for a moment in his eyes. Trying to keep her voice from shaking, she said, 'Yes, about that.'

'And yet another coincidence that you should be in Lisbon on business just as Carina finds it necessary to come here, too,' Luis pointed out acidly.

'Yes, a very happy coincidence,' Greg agreed, and drew himself up challengingly.

Carina looked at the two men, both tall but otherwise so completely different. Greg, in his white tuxedo and with his white-blond hair. Luis, so dark in comparison in his black evening-suit, the whiteness of his shirt accentuating his dark hair and eyes, and the deepness of his inborn Mediterranean tan. To her strained mind, they seemed like the white knight and the black knight—and everyone knew who always won out of those two.

Quickly, to break the tension, Carina said, 'Did you phone the villa? Was Stella there?'

Luis's eyes flicked back to her, cold and withdrawn again now. 'No. My housekeeper told me that she went out this afternoon and was going straight on to her place of work. And it seems that she doesn't get back until very late at night, so I left a message for her to phone me tomorrow morning.'

'At what time? I should like to be there when she rings.'

'I dare say you would, but I'm not going to let you coerce Stella against her wishes.'

'I don't intend to coerce her,' Carina returned angrily. 'I only want to ...'

She broke off as a woman came up to them, smiled, and spoke to Carina in Portuguese, asking her to tell Greg how keen her teenage son was on golf, and inviting them both to dinner at her house the following evening.

When she'd finished, Luis began to say. 'Perhaps I could translate for you ...'

But Carina said shortly, 'That isn't necessary,' and turned to give Greg the woman's words, almost verbatim.

'Tell her that's kind of her, but I've already been invited out tomorrow. But tell her, also, that I'll leave a signed copy of my book at the reception desk in my hotel for her son, if he'd like to come round and collect it some time,' Greg added good-naturedly.

As Carina interpreted for him, she was very aware of Luis listening intently, his attention betraying his surprise at her fluency.

Senhora Alvor, their hostess, came over to join them, and for a few minutes there was general conversation, but then she drew Greg away to talk to some other people, the other woman going with them.

Carina went to follow, but Luis put a hand on her arm and held her back. The unexpected touch of his fingers on her bare skin sent a shock-wave jarring through her veins and Carina couldn't have moved if she'd tried. Slowly, she turned her head to look at him.

'Your Portuguese seems to have improved considerably since you left,' he commented drily.

Pulling her arm free, Carina took a step away from him. She felt numbed by her reactions to his touch, so that her face was set and her tone very short as she said, 'I'd had so many lessons here, I thought I might as well make some use of them. It seemed silly to let it all go to waste.'

Luis's jaw tightened. 'I'm glad that our marriage wasn't a complete waste of time, then,' he said in bitter sarcasm.

'I didn't mean ...' Carina shrugged mentally. What did it matter? Let him think what he liked.

What he was thinking became obvious when Luis said, 'And I suppose you thought it would be amusing to—to . . .' For a moment, his English deserted him. 'To flaunt your lover in front of my business associates?'

'I didn't know they were your associates. I didn't even know you knew them. How could I?'

'But you don't deny that he's your lover,' Luis said tersely, anger again in his eyes.

'It's a remark I choose to ignore. Anyway,' she retorted coldly, stung to anger herself, 'it's none of your business.'

Reaching out, Luis caught her wrist, his angry fingers biting into her skin as he said in a harsh voice, made the more menacing because it was spoken in an undertone, 'Yes, it is. While you're my wife and in my country, then it *is* my business.'

Carina would have liked to throw the contents of her glass of wine in his face. Once, years ago, when they'd had a fight, she had done. But it was the memory of the way Luis had retaliated on that occasion, as much as anything, that held her back now. Instead, she drew herself up, her green eyes flashing fire, and said as disdainfully as she knew how, 'Really, you're becoming ridiculous! As if it mattered now.' And she turned and walked over to the group around Greg, slipped her arm through his and smiled up at him.

Seeing the brilliant smile, Greg correctly guessed that something was wrong and bent to say in her ear, 'Do you want to leave?'

'Yes, definitely,' she hissed back.

He didn't waste any time. Within five minutes, he'd apologised to their hosts, stressing how tired they were after the journey, had a taxi called, and they were saying goodbye. As they did so, Luis came out into the hall. 'Going already?' he remarked. 'Let me give you a lift; I'm going back into the city.'

'Thanks, but we already have a taxi on the way,' Greg answered shortly.

'Until tomorrow, then,' Luis answered easily. He nodded to Carina, but made no attempt to shake hands with either of them, instead turning to say goodnight to the Alvors.

The taxi came, and Luis almost immediately followed them out of the house, getting into a car parked further down the street. His headlights followed them down the hill, and were then swallowed up by the other traffic as they entered the busy main streets, but Carina had the prickly feeling that Luis was still behind them. Following to see if they were both staying at the same hotel, Carina thought indignantly.

'So *that* was your husband,' Greg remarked. 'He wasn't what I expected.'

'No? What did you expect?'

'I don't really know. But not someone as hard as that. Or as cool.'

Carina looked at him in surprise. Couldn't he see how angry Luis was behind that cold exterior? To her, it had been more than obvious. But then, she happened to know Luis rather well.

'That man he's representing—I think he must have phoned Luis—told him I was there. I'm sorry.'

'Not to worry,' Greg said easily. 'Who's this girl you were talking about?'

'Stella? She's my sister. She's the main reason I'm over here.' And she told Greg all about it.

'So you're not really sure if you'll be going down to

the Algarve tomorrow?'

'Oh, I shall definitely go. Whether Luis says that Stella agrees or not.'

'And what about your divorce? Has Riveiro agreed to give you one?'

Carina shook her head. 'He says he doesn't want one.'

'Doesn't want one? But that's crazy! Unless he thinks you'll get back together.'

'That's quite impossible,' Carina said firmly. 'But in a strange way I feel as he does. As I don't want to get married again, there doesn't seem much point in going through all the trauma of getting a divorce.'

Greg glanced at her and picked up her hand. 'Are you very tired?'

'No. Not really.'

'Then how about having a nightcap somewhere? Does your hotel have a bar?'

'No, I don't think so. It's only a small place.'

'Mine has. Shall we go there and have a drink? Unless you know of somewhere else?'

Carina thought but didn't really know any bars. They weren't the kind of place that Luis had ever taken her to. If they had gone out into the city, it had always been for a show or a meal. 'No, that would be fine.'

So Greg redirected the taxi and they went into his hotel together. It wasn't all that late, and there were still several people in the bar, sitting over their drinks. They found a quiet corner and Greg ordered, then sat back and said, 'It seems that we're becoming rather involved, doesn't it? Why did you want your husband to think that we'd known each other longer?'

Her cheeks flushing slightly, Carina said, 'I just didn't want him to know that you'd—er—picked me up only this morning, that's all.'

'We *met* this morning,' Greg corrected her. 'It wasn't a pick-up. We met, we liked each other, and we wanted to see each other again. It was that simple. At least, it was for me.' And he raised an eyebrow interrogatively.

'And for me,' Carina agreed with a smile. 'But my life is complicated at the moment, and I don't want to involve you in my troubles, so I . . .'

'But maybe I want to be involved,' Greg interrupted. 'And, anyway, as I said, I am already. Don't forget, I shall be connected with your husband in the holiday development.'

'But only very remotely.' Leaning towards him, Carina said earnestly, 'Look, Greg, I've enjoyed your company, but I really feel that it would be better if we didn't see each other again.'

His eyebrows rose. 'Is that a polite way of telling me to mind my own business?'

'It just wouldn't be fair to complicate your life with my problems,' she answered shortly.

'You *are* telling me to mind my own business.'

'No, but I . . .' She looked at him rather helplessly.

Taking her left hand in his, Greg said, 'Why aren't you wearing a wedding ring?'

'Because I don't feel married any more, I suppose.'

'So why don't you want to get a divorce and be completely free of him?'

Carina shrugged rather helplessly. 'I don't really know.'

'It couldn't be because you're still in love with him, could it?' Greg asked, his eyes intent on her face.

'Oh, no!' She shook her head decisively, then pondered for a moment. 'I suppose it's mostly because it's so difficult to admit that you were once so stupid, that you made such a terrible mistake. When Luis, and the life I had with him for such a short time, was so far away, then I could almost believe that it never happened. It's coming back here and seeing him again that has brought it all so close.'

'Well, maybe it's a good thing that you're having to face up to it. Maybe you were drifting before.'

Carina nodded reflectively. 'Perhaps you're right. It's easy to just drift along, isn't it?' Her voice fell to a low murmur, as if she'd forgotten Greg was there. 'Sometimes it all seems as if it was just a bad dream.'

Turning her hand, Greg began to play idly with her fingers. 'You know, Carina, it seems to me that you might need some help while you're going through this. I was some help tonight, wasn't I?'

'Yes, of course. I'm very grateful. But . . .'

He put a finger over her lips. 'No buts. I *want* to help. I want to get to know you better. So promise me you'll let me know when you leave Lisbon, and you'll give me an address where I can contact you on the Algarve.'

Carina looked at him, her eyes smiling. 'Are you in the habit of extracting promises from all the women you meet?' she asked flippantly.

'No, only from the ones I'm frightened of losing.'

'I'm flattered!' she mocked teasingly.

Greg grinned. 'You should be.' And, leaning forward, he kissed her very lightly on the lips, his eyes open and holding hers.

Carina gazed back for a long moment, then took a deep breath. 'On that note,' she said huskily, 'I think I'd better go.'

Greg laughed as he stood up. 'I'll take you back to your hotel.'

'No, that's OK. Just see me into a taxi.'

As they walked towards the entrance, he said, 'I told you—no strings.'

'No, I know. But it isn't worth you coming back with me. I'll be all right alone.'

'It *is* worth it,' Greg corrected. 'But I'll let you go by yourself.' The doorman whistled for a taxi, and Greg put her into it, giving the driver money for the fare. 'Don't forget to phone me tomorrow.'

'I won't. Thanks for tonight—and for backing me up.'

'Any time. Goodnight, Carina.' He went to close the door, but then, almost as if he was compelled to do so, he leaned in and put his hand behind her neck, kissing her hard on the mouth. Quickly then, Greg stepped back, closed the door, and stood on the pavement, his eyes following the taxi until it was out of sight.

CHAPTER THREE

LUIS rang at nine-thirty the following morning. By that time Carina was up, had breakfasted, and was all packed, ready to leave.

'I've been in touch with Stella,' Luis said brusquely, and without even saying good morning first. 'She's willing to see you.'

'Is that how she put it—or how you're putting it?' Carina asked icily, offended by his tone.

'She's willing to talk to you, isn't that enough? She will be at the villa all day today, if you want to phone her.'

'No, I'll go straight down there and talk to her in person.'

'As you wish. I'll let them know you're coming, so that the housekeeper can get a room ready.'

'*No!*' Carina said forcefully, adding more calmly, 'Thank you, but I prefer to stay in a hotel.'

'Why?'

The direct question completely disconcerted her. 'Because I do, that's all.'

'Why don't you come right out and say it?' Luis demanded harshly. 'You don't want to stay at the villa, because you want to stay at a hotel with your lover. Isn't that so?'

'No, it is not,' Carina retorted in a white heat of anger. 'I don't want to stay at your villa, because I want nothing more to do with you. And I especially don't

53

want any favours from you.'

'No? That wasn't what you said yesterday, when you asked me to help find Stella.'

'That was on Stella's and my mother's behalf, not my own. Personally, I'd hoped never to see or speak to you again. As far as I'm concerned,' she added, intending to hurt, 'you're just one of those bad experiences one tries to forget as soon as possible.'

There was a short, shattering silence, before Luis's voice came over the line again, savage in its anger. 'Perhaps you could at least have the decency to show some discretion in your affair with Summers. You still bear my name, and I would prefer not to have it dragged in the dirt all over the Algarve.'

He slammed the phone down then, but Carina could almost imagine how he looked; his mouth set and sneering, jaw thrust arrogantly forward, and fierce rage burning in his dark eyes. Her hand shaking, she replaced the receiver and sat for a moment, trying to recover. Luis always had been possessive, and at the beginning that had been fun, she'd enjoyed it. But later, when life in Lisbon had started to become hellish, Carina had become friendly with some young English people who attended the same language course as she did. One day, Luis had seen her in a café with a couple of the male students, and she had been amazed at the angry jealousy he'd shown. And it seemed as if he was still jealous even now, even though they'd lived separate lives for so long.

Deciding that the best thing to do would be to put as much distance as possible between Luis and herself, Carina got briskly to her feet. She had already arranged to hire a car, and within half an hour she was threading her way out of Lisbon and across a huge bridge over the

River Tagus, the bridge they called April the Twenty-Fifth to commemorate the 1974 *coup d'état*. It was the longest suspension bridge in Europe, and overlooked what must be the most beautiful scenery, with the city dominated by castles and spires behind her, and ahead the huge statue of Christ with arms outspread that towered into the sky on the opposite bank.

Carina had hired a convertible car and, as she motored along the *autostrada*, the sun on her head, her spirits gradually lifted and she felt almost happy. Because she was getting away from Luis? Definitely. And also away from any possible complications with Greg? Possibly. She decided to forget about both men and just concentrate on what she'd come to do: seeing Stella and persuading her to go home. And maybe she would try to do some sunbathing too. It had been ages since she'd had a holiday. Looking at the pale skin of her arms, Carina decided to get her priorities right; she definitely needed a tan.

The *autostrada* soon degenerated into a very poor main road, it wasn't even dual carriageway, and Carina kept getting stuck behind lorries lumbering their way down to the Algarve. But if the going was slow the scenery made up for it. She passed fields of commercially grown sunflowers, the tall-stalked flowers turning their huge yellow heads to follow the sun. Then there were row upon row of cork trees, many of them with half the bark stripped from their trunks, leaving bare orange patches that would grow over, so that in a few years they could be stripped again. She drove through a range of hills, and down through small towns, where the road became narrow and twisted, the tarmac giving way to cobbles, the peace to the blare of car horns. With each

kilometre she travelled from Lisbon, so Carina felt as if
she was leaving the hurry and pace of the late twentieth
century behind and going back in time.

At last she reached the Algarve, as far south as she
could go, where peasants still rode on pannier-laden
donkeys, and scratched a living from the arid soil.

It was much more difficult to find a room than Carina
had expected. The holiday season had already started,
and it seemed that most of the hotels had had their rooms
pre-booked by big holiday companies. In the end, she
managed to find a vacancy in the only hotel in a small
fishing village about six miles from Luis's villa, but she
had to take a double room as they hadn't any singles
available. Here she had a quick shower, and a meal in a
café on the beach, before setting out again to see her
sister.

When Carina had stayed at the villa with Luis on their
honeymoon, nearly five years ago, the house had been
run very ably by a plump, middle-aged house-keeper
called Almeira, who came in every weekday, going home
to her own house not far away in the evenings. The villa
stood on the side of a hill, looking out over the sea, and
had once been the only house of any size in the area, with
a path leading down through a subsidence in the cliffs to
its own private beach. But now villas and holiday
developments were mushrooming along the coast, the
new houses painted stark white and roofed with bright
red pantiles, spreading outwards from every port and
fishing village. The last development had reached within
half a mile of the villa, but it was still screened by trees,
orange, lemon and the tall cypresses that stood like dark
sentinels against the intensely blue sky. Carina turned
into a twisting, climbing driveway and tried not to

remember the first time she'd ever gone there with Luis.

The villa was a dull stone colour that didn't dazzle one's eyes, the roof tiles mellowed by the sun and toning in with the landscape. But there was colour everywhere, in the flowers that grew riotously in the garden and cascaded in great falls of mauve and red over the veranda and roof. When Carina got slowly out of the car, she stood for a moment, drinking in the scents, scents that evoked so many memories that she shut her eyes, her heart suddenly aching and raw.

'Hello, big sister.'

Stella's voice from the veranda made Carina open her eyes and come back to the present. 'Hello, yourself.' Her eyes ran over her sister's figure. 'Well, at least you're still in one piece.'

'Did you doubt it?'

'Mother did.'

Stella grimaced, and ran down the steps to give Carina a hug. 'She would. Have you come all this way just because of Mum making a fuss?'

'You're not exactly a good correspondent, you know. All we got from you in months were cryptic postcards.'

She would have said more, but a woman came out of the house and Carina gave a smile of pleasure. 'Almeira!'

'*Senhora!* What a pleasure to see you again.' The older woman ran down the steps and clasped Carina's hand in both of hers. 'I knew that one day you would come back again. You and Senhor Luis, you have so much love for one another, I knew you would come back to him.'

Carina's eyes shadowed and she tried to speak, but it was impossible to break through the maid's voluble greetings. Better to leave it for the present, she decided, and explain later when she could get Almeira alone and talk to her in Portuguese.

'But where are your cases?' the maid asked, looking in the car.

'I don't have any, I'm not staying. But I'd love one of your fresh orange drinks, if I may.'

'Of course. At once.' The frown on Almeira's face cleared as she hurried away.

'Why aren't you staying here?' Stella asked, as she led the way to a table and sun loungers set out on the end of a terrace overlooking the pool.

'This is Luis's house, remember?'

'How did it go, seeing him again?' Stella asked, her voice agog with curiosity.

Carina gave her a suspicious look. At almost nineteen, Stella was a more rounded and darker-gold version of herself. She had the same shape of face and eyebrows, but her eyes were hazel, whereas Carina's were that cool shade of green that could look like deep glacial ice. 'How do you expect?' Carina shrugged. 'We were neither of us overjoyed. And I wasn't that pleased to find out that you'd been writing to him all these years.'

'Oh, he told you that, did he?'

'He did. Just what did you tell him about me?'

The younger girl laughed. 'Wouldn't you like to know?'

Carina gave a theatrical shudder. 'I hate to think. When I remember some of the wimps I went out with on the rebound ...'

'Well, you would go out with men who were as different from Luis as you could find.' Sitting up, Stella undid the top of her bikini and dropped it on the floor.

She was completely brown underneath, without any strap-marks.

'You'll shock Almeira,' Carina warned.

'Don't be silly, I always sunbathe like this. Why don't you change? Did you bring a bikini with you?'

'I did. In fact, I'm wearing it.' And Carina took off her sundress to reveal a brief white bikini.

'You have such a gorgeous figure,' Stella complained enviously. 'Will I ever be as slim as you?'

'Not the way you usually laze around all day,' her sister returned heartlessly.

Almeira came out with the drinks, and they chatted about her family for half an hour or so, until the maid left to go home.

Lying back in her lounger, Carina closed her eyes, content to soak up the sun, but presently she said, 'You're still very fond of Luis, aren't you?'

'Why shouldn't I be? I always thought he was fantastic, and just because you fell out of love with him ...'

'It's all right, I'm not knocking it,' Carina soothed. 'It was just an observation, that's all.'

'He's my brother-in-law,' Stella said defensively. 'If *I'd* been married to him, I'd never have left him.'

'*You* didn't have to live with his mother and father,' Carina pointed out tartly.

There was no answer to that, and the two girls fell silent again until Carina said reluctantly, 'In your postcard you said that you'd met someone—is that still on?'

'Why do you want to know?'

'Oh, for heaven's sake, Stell! You know the way that Mother's mind works. She immediately thought that you were going to follow my unedifying example. Having one daughter who shattered all her hopes is bad enough. To have two . . .'

'If ever I go back to England,' Stella said musingly, 'I'm not going to live at home any more.'

'Good for you. You can live with me when you're not at university, if you like.'

Stella stood up. 'Oh, that's only if I decide to go back to England. I'm not at all sure that I want to yet.' And she stepped to the edge of the pool and did a neat dive into its inviting waters.

No matter how much she tried, Carina couldn't get anything more out of her that day. They went out to dinner that evening, and Carina ordered wine, because Stella usually opened up more when she'd had a few drinks, but tonight she was like a clam, refusing to even say a word about the man she'd met. At ten, Carina dropped Stella off at the villa and drove back to her hotel, still none the wiser and feeling decidedly annoyed and frustrated.

Stella had to work the next day, so Carina, with a sigh of exasperation, sat down in her hotel bedroom to do battle with the terrible Portuguese phone system. First, she decided to telephone Greg in Lisbon, eventually getting through to his hotel to learn that he was out, but getting cut off twice before she was able to leave a message telling him where she was staying. Then she tried to phone her mother in England, and to do that she had to just keep trying the number again and again in the hope of picking up a free overseas line. But after an hour of this, Carina gave up and went down to the hotel pool to sunbathe and try and relax. After the efficiency of the British phone system, it was difficult to remember that she was in Portugal now. Here, everything was on a different wavelength, and she had to realise that there was just no point in getting uptight about anything as trivial as an inefficient telephone system. Getting annoyed wasn't going to make any difference. Just take it as it comes, she told herself, and lay back to soak up Portugal's greatest asset—those endless hours of glorious sunshine.

That evening, Carina again tried to get through to her mother, but gave up after half an hour, and drove to Albufeira to look for the bar where Stella was working. She found it in one of the twisting roads leading down towards the fish market and the beach, a nondescript looking place with a bar and tables inside, mainly for the locals, and tables and chairs outside for thirsty passing tourists.

Carina sat down at an empty table, and after a couple of minutes Stella came out with a tray of drinks for another table. 'Checking up on me?' she asked tartly when she came over.

'I've nowhere else to go,' Carina pointed out. 'So I thought I might as well come here. After all, you did tell me how to find it.'

Stella nodded, but twisted her mouth wryly. 'Would you like a drink?'

'Please. Something long and cool.'

From where Carina was sitting, she could see all the outside tables and also into the bar. She had figured that Stella's boyfriend, whoever he was, would either be working at the bar, too, or would be hanging around it. There were four youths, English, by the sound of it, sitting at one of the outside tables, but none of these, or anyone else at the bar, looked like someone Stella would go mad about. Carina sat on, hoping the mysterious boyfriend would show up, but after a couple of hours just couldn't stomach any more drinks and went for a meal instead, picking Stella up at ten o'clock to drive her to the villa.

'Would you like to come in for a nightcap?' Stella offered.

Carina groaned inwardly at the thought of another drink, but decided that she ought to take any opportunity to talk with Stella, in the hope that the younger girl would confide in her. So she went into the villa, and wandered round while Stella had a shower and changed. She pushed open the door of the master bedroom, the one that Luis's parents had always used and which still contained the big, old-fashioned furniture that they favoured. It was very clean, but it had an unlived-in look, and Carina guessed that it hadn't been used for some time. Stella was using one of the guest bedrooms, and the other stood in shuttered darkness. Which left only Luis's room, the one that they had shared on their honeymoon. Slowly, Carina pushed open the door, and turned on a lamp.

It was like stepping back in time. She remembered so vividly that first night together, when Luis had picked her up in his arms to carry her across the threshold of this room ...

Eagerly he shouldered open the door and pushed it shut behind them, shutting the world and all their problems outside. His shadowed face was taut with excitement and anticipation, his eyes burning with desire. Setting her down on her feet, Luis turned on the lamp, and then he put his hands on either side of her face, his eyes devouring each feature before he bent to softly touch her lips, and then crush her to him as he took her mouth in a fever of rapturous passion. His hands went to her clothes, tearing them in his eagerness, throwing them on to the floor, until his hands were on her skin, so hot, so avid in their caresses. He spoke words of passionate endearment, his voice thick and ragged; no silent lover, he. Picking her up, he carried her the few feet to the bed, then stripped off his own clothes and slid down beside her. It seemed to Carina, then, that he loved her with every part of him; his eyes, his lips, his voice, his hands, even his skin seemed to touch her with love, until she was enveloped in it, engulfed, drowning in its density and fierceness.

And she, too, was on fire with hunger for Luis. Even now, the room seemed to echo with her moans of pleasure, her cries, first of pain and then of rapture . . .

Again and again, she gasped out his name. 'Luis, my love, my darling. I love you! I love you!' She clung to his sweat-soaked body, terrified, and yet wanting this more than anything she had ever wanted in the world. He tried to be gentle, but his hunger for her was so great that he took her in a savage blaze of passion, taking possession of her body with a fierce need that couldn't be denied, and lifting her with him to the heights of dizzy ecstasy.

Afterwards, he groaned and said, '*Sorry! Sorry* I hurt you.' But she wouldn't have had it any other way. She had *wanted* him to take her with hunger and unbridled ardour, wanted to know that she had given herself to a man of fire and passion, a man to whom making love was an overpowering need, and not an acquired technique.

That he had needed her, Luis proved several times more that night, until they fell into exhausted sleep in one another's arms, not waking till the sunlight streamed through the windows the next morning, enveloping them its golden warmth ...

'Carina? Are you all right?'

Stella's voice brought Carina back to reality. She found that she was leaning back against the wall, her eyes tightly closed, and her fists pressed against her mouth. Straightening up, she said hastily, 'Yes. Yes, of course. I'm fine.' But she had to put up a finger to wipe a surreptitious tear from the corner of her eye.

'Was this your room? Yours and Luis's?'

'Yes.' Stepping past her, Carina walked into the sitting-room. 'You offered me a drink.'

'Yes, of course. What would you like?'

'Gin and tonic, please. With lots of ice.'

Stella poured it for her and Carina took a long swallow, needing it now. Then she said abruptly, 'This man you've met—do you think that you're in love with him?'

'Think?'

'It could be just infatuation,' Carina pointed out. 'Only time will give you the answer to that.'

'Are you saying that what you felt for Luis was only infatuation?'

'That's a very personal question.'

'So was yours,' Stella retorted, in no way put down.

'My marriage to Luis was a mistake.'

'That doesn't answer my question.'

Carina gave her sister a hard look. 'What are you up to, Stell? If you think that Luis and I might get back together, you couldn't be more wrong.'

'Why should I think that?'

'Because you always were a romantic. And that's why

I'm frightened for you now.' Taking hold of the younger girl's hand, Carina said urgently, 'Please, don't make the same mistake I did. A broken marriage is absolute hell, believe me. Look, this man—this boy that you've met, try and get him out of your system. Even go to bed with him, if you must, but get him out of your mind so that you can go back to England and go to university like you planned.'

'Mother would have a thousand fits if she heard you advising me to go to bed with someone,' Stella said on a high, rather nervous laugh.

'Mother isn't here. And she doesn't understand.'

'Is that why you married Luis so quickly?' the younger girl asked curiously. 'To get away from Mother?'

'No.' Carina moved away so that Stella couldn't see her face. 'I married Luis because that was what he wanted. If he'd just wanted me to go to bed with him, I would have done that willingly, but he wanted marriage.' Looking down at her glass, she said slowly, 'Maybe it would have been better if we'd gone to bed first, got the sexual side of it out of the way. Then we could have got to know each other and the—the conditions we'd have to live in before we committed ourselves.' She smiled, a brittle smile of irony. 'But Luis had a puritan streak in him. He was in love and it had to be marriage.'

'So for Luis, at least, it was love,' Stella said softly. 'It must have been quite a shock for him, having you walk into his office like that.'

'How do you know that's what I did?'

'He told me on the phone.'

'Was that—all he said?' Carina asked, wondering if he'd passed on any details about Greg.

But it seemed he hadn't, because Stella said, 'Only that you were looking for me and did I want to see you?'

'But you know why, don't you? Please, Stella, give this man up and come home. We can leave tomorrow—drive into Spain, if you like. I've arranged to take some time off, and we can have a holiday together for another couple of weeks before we need go back to England,' she wheedled.

'You make it sound as if you're the one who's in a hurry to get away,' Stella remarked. 'Are you running away from Luis again, Carina?'

Draining her glass, Carina set it down on a table and walked towards the door. 'Are you working tomorrow?'

'Yes, but only in the morning.'

'OK, why don't I pick you up and we'll have lunch together? Bring your swimsuit, and we'll find a beach somewhere.' She paused. 'Unless you've made other plans, of course.'

'No, I haven't made any plans for tomorrow.'

Stella's answer puzzled Carina somewhat as she drove back to the hotel. Just when was this mysterious boyfriend going to show up? she wondered. Unless, of course, Stella was purposely keeping him hidden away until Carina gave up and went home. Carina thought about it all the way home, and it wasn't until she was getting ready for bed that something else that had been hovering in her subconscious came back into her mind. She had been so overcome by memories when she had looked into their old bedroom, that it only now registered that that room, too, had had an unlived-in look, as if Luis had obliterated every trace of himself from it and hadn't used it since she'd gone away.

* * *

The next morning, Carina waited until Stella would be safely at work and then drove over to the villa again to talk to Almeira, reluctantly going behind her sister's back to try and find out who her boyfriend was. If she'd taken him back to the villa, Almeira would be bound to know about it, one way or the other, and Carina hoped that the maid had enough good sense to reveal what she knew. But again Carina drew a blank. Almeira was more than happy to gossip, but it was soon evident that Stella had only brought friends there on two occasions, both in daytime, and both times bringing a small crowd of young people who had swam in the pool and then all left together.

'And Senhor Luis and his mother?' Carina couldn't resist asking. 'Do they often come to stay now?'

'Oh, no,' Almeira shook her head regretfully. 'Senhora Riveiro has not been here since she has been ill. Over a year now. And Senhor Luis, he does not come at all.'

Carina gave her a startled look; having convinced herself that her thought of the night before had been only a foolish piece of imagination, she felt it as quite a shock to have it confirmed.

She left soon afterwards to pick up Stella, and after lunch they drove to a beach where, like everyone else, they took off their bikini tops and sunbathed on the smooth, soft sands. Afterwards, they met up with some other young people that Stella knew, and they all went on to a disco, but none of the boys showed any marked partiality for Stella nor she for them, so that didn't help. All Carina could get out of her was a promise to spend the day with her again tomorrow. 'But don't come to the villa too early,' Stella told her. 'I like to sleep late on

Saturday mornings.'

Probably because it was the weekend and the lines weren't so busy, Carina managed to telephone her mother the next morning, after trying for only half an hour. She gave the good news first, telling her that she had found Stella, and tried to make the news sound better than it was by saying that she was trying to persuade her sister to take a holiday in Spain with her. That duty done, Carina gave a sigh of relief and drove over to the villa, stopping at a market on the way where she bought thin slices of lean ham, fat red tomatoes and fruit for lunch. She wore only yellow shorts and a matching suntop, with yellow rope-soled espadrilles on her feet; her hair fell loose and blew around her head as she drove along with the roof down. With the sun shining so brightly, it was impossible not to feel good and almost carefree, so that Carina blew a fanfare on the horn as she drew up outside the villa.

'Hey!' she shouted, collecting her shopping from the car and going on to the veranda. 'Wake up! I've brought lunch.' There was no answering shout so Carina walked round the house to the terrace overlooking the pool. Two loungers had been set out, but Stella wasn't there. Still in bed, Carina thought with a grin. Putting her shopping bags down, she began to walk towards the back of the house, intending to hammer on Stella's shutters until she woke up. But as she neared the corner she heard the sound of the patio doors on to the terrace being slid open and turned back. 'Oh, so you *are* up. I was just about to ...' Carina's voice died in her throat and she stood quite still as, not her sister, but Luis, stepped through the doors.

The surprise was total. It was as much of a shock for

her to see him as it must have been for Luis when she'd
turned up at his office. But at least he had had a few
minutes to compose himself before they actually came
face to face. Carina had none. Her eyes betrayed her the
most, growing wide and vulnerable. Her lips parted in
surprise, but she didn't speak; she could only stare at
him for the few moments that it took for her heart to
start beating again, as if the world had stood still for
long, shattering seconds.

Somehow Carina found her voice and said, 'Good
morning,' in a cold, withdrawn tone that was still in
shock.

'Good morning,' Luis replied taking a couple of steps
towards her. 'You seem surprised to see me.'

'I was expecting Stella. And besides . . .'

She stopped, but Luis raised an interrogative eyebrow. 'Besides?'

'Almeira said that you never came here any more,'
Carina admitted reluctantly.

'So you asked her, did you?' Luis said mockingly.

'Of course. Obviously, I didn't want to run into you if
I could possibly avoid it,' she hit back. Luis's jaw
tightened dangerously and Carina drew a deep breath,
trying to recover herself. 'Why have you come down
now? To make sure I haven't kidnapped Stella, I
suppose. Where is she, anyway? Not still in bed, surely?'

'She isn't here. When I arrived half an hour ago, I
found a note she had left on the kitchen table, saying that
she would be back in time for lunch.' His eyes were
going over her as he spoke, taking in the long line of her
bare legs, the suntop that she'd knotted under her
breasts to leave her midriff bare, and her shining
dishevelled hair.

'Did Stella know you were coming?' Carina demanded, turning abruptly away.

'Yes, I rang and told her.'

Damn! Carina swore inwardly. No wonder Stella had
made herself scarce. 'She didn't tell me. When are you
leaving?'

'Either Sunday night or early Monday.'

'Then perhaps you would tell Stella that I'll see her at
the bar where she works, some time on Monday.'
Picking up her bag, Carina began to walk away.

'I thought you came to lunch?' Luis remarked,
following her.

'I did—but I've suddenly lost my appetite.'

'You always were a coward,' Luis said sardonically as
she reached her car.

Turning to face him, Carina said coldly, 'I'm not
afraid of you, if that's what you mean.'

'So why are you running away?'

'Because I can think of better things to do with my
time than spend them in your company,' she retorted.

'But your boyfriend is still in Lisbon,' Luis pointed
out sneeringly. 'Surely he let you know?'

Greg had, in fact, left a couple of messages at the
hotel, asking her to call him, but she hadn't done so. 'If
you mean Greg Summers,' she said frostily, 'he's been
in touch with me.'

'Oh, I'm *quite* sure he has,' Luis said with such
insolent mockery that she got the meaning at once.

Her face white, she said, 'I don't have to take that
from you. I'll do what I damn well like—with *whoever* I
like. And don't try to tell me that you haven't been with
other women since we broke up, because I won't believe
you!' she added angrily. 'You're much too sexually

active to . . .' She stopped abruptly, realising what she was saying.

Luis grinned broadly, the first time she'd seen him smile for over four years. 'So that, at least, you remember.'

'I remember everything,' she answered shortly. 'The tears, the oppression, the fights . . .' She stopped and shot him a look of bitter irony. 'Just like the one we're having now.'

His eyebrows drawing together into a frown, Luis said, 'You're right. I'm sorry.' He gestured with his hand. 'Look, don't run—don't leave. Let's at least try to talk without arguing. Come and sit down. Have a drink.'

'We have nothing to talk about.'

'Yes, we do. There's Stella. Has she agreed to go back to England with you?'

'Haven't you asked her yourself?'

'No. I didn't think I had the right to ask.'

'I'm surprised she hasn't confided in you,' Carina said on a biting note. 'You and she being so chummy all this time.'

Luis gave her a long look and put out a hand to take her arm, but Carina moved out of the way. His mouth twisted a little, but he merely said, 'Let's go and sit down.'

She gave him a swift glance, then nodded reluctantly. 'All right. But only for a few minutes.' She sat on one of the loungers by the pool, while Luis went inside to make some drinks. It gave them both a short breathing space, so that they were more composed, if still angry, when Luis came out to join her.

'Have you persuaded Stella?' he asked again as he sat on the other lounger.

'No, not yet. She hasn't even told me who her boyfriend is. It seems that we don't have quite the close relationship that I thought,' she added wryly.

'It's her first time on her own. Perhaps she's enjoying her independence and doesn't want to give it up.'

'Possibly,' Carina agreed. 'But she never used to be—secretive before. We could always talk, and she used to confide in me.'

'And did you confide in her?'

Carina was silent for a moment, then shook her head. 'Not about anything that really mattered.'

'Did you tell her about us?'

Leaning forward, Carina searched in her bag for her dark glasses and put them on. 'Is that a roundabout way of asking if you mattered?'

'We're married,' he pointed out. 'I could hardly not matter.'

'Do you want to go through it all again? Is that what this is all about?'

'Maybe it might help to get it out of our systems,' Luis answered carefully. 'We might even discover where we went wrong.'

'What would be the point? Our marriage is over, and neither of us seems to have any inclination to try it again.' She gave a harsh laugh. 'Who in their right mind would want to? I certainly don't!'

Luis stood up, his body tense. 'And what about Greg Summers? You're obviously having an affair with him. Or isn't he offering marriage?' he asked sardonically. 'Does he prefer you to be married? Does it make him feel safe?'

Carina came angrily to her feet and faced him, tearing

off her glasses. 'No,' she returned furiously, 'it makes *me* feel safe!'

They stood facing each other between the two loungers, only a couple of feet apart, both taut with anger. Suddenly, Luis reached out and grabbed her arm. 'Can't you see what you're doing?' he demanded. 'See what you're becoming?'

'It's nothing to do with you! I don't . . .'

'*Oh yes, it damn well is.*' And, dragging her to him, Luis put his hand behind her head and kissed her.

'No!' But there was no time to protest further as his mouth took hers in a compulsive need that wanted only to master her, to dominate and possess all over again. His lips bruised hers as he bent her head back, forceful, angry, using his strength to bend her to his will, to make her capitulate. Carina's first reaction was to fight him, and for a few moments she struggled in his hold. But this only seemed to anger him further, and she realised that it was a struggle she could never win. So she became very still, holding herself as rigidly as she could beneath the violation of her mouth.

As soon as Luis realised what she was doing his kisses became more insistent, more insinuating. His lips left her mouth to trace a hot path along her chin and neck, down her throat and across her shoulder. Carina stood perfectly still, her eyes closed, trying to still the turmoil in her heart, trying not to let him know what his touch, his nearness, his lips, were doing to her. It had been so long since a kiss had meant anything, since a man's touch had set her skin on fire, since anyone had roused this pain of need and emptiness deep in her body.

His lips came back to her mouth, persistently seeking a response, and he murmured her name deep in his throat, as his hands pushed aside the straps of her suntop.

Oh God, how can my body betray me like this? Carina groaned inwardly. It had been so long. Her body *ached* to be held and touched. She wanted to press herself against him, to feel his hard body enter hers as it had so often and so wonderfully in the past. She wanted ... With a cry of revulsion, Carina tore herself from his arms.

'Get away from me!' she yelled at him. 'Can't you see that I don't want you? Why won't you get it into your head—you're my past, Luis, not my future. I don't want you or your big Latin-lover act. It may have turned me on once, but it doesn't do anything for me now. You're out of date, Luis,' she told him cruelly. 'You're the past tense!'

His face grim, he caught hold of her again. 'I suppose you prefer Summers. Is he so marvellous a lover, then?'

'*Yes*,' she answered fiercely. 'Yes, I prefer him. He doesn't make demands on me like you do—did.'

But Luis was too angry to notice her slip. With a snarl, he said, 'No, and that's why you don't love him, why you'll never marry him. Because with him you'll never come alive as you did with me. In my arms, you were a wild thing, a creature of love and passion. As you never could be with any other man. And you know it! However much you try to deny it, even to yourself, you will never love or be loved by anyone else as you were with me.'

CHAPTER FOUR

CARINA gave him a glaring look of cold fury and ran to the car. This time, Luis didn't try to stop her. Her hands were shaking so much that it took her several seconds to sort out the key and get it into the ignition. As the engine burst into life, she looked up and saw Luis was watching, his face grim and set. Angrily, she gunned the accelerator and spun the wheel to turn and plunge down the steep driveway, her only thought to get as far away from Luis as possible. She shot round the last bend before the entrance—and stood on the brakes to avoid hitting Stella, who was walking up the middle of the drive! Carina's body was jerked forward against the steering wheel, and her head and shoulder hit the windscreen, but she managed to stop in time, the back wheels skidding against the tarmac. The engine had stalled, and for a minute there was a ghastly silence until Stella, who had stood frozen as the car came towards her, recovered enough to run to the side of the car.

'My God, Carina, I thought you were going to run me down! Why on earth were you going so fast? I ...' Reaching forward, she touched her sister's shoulder. 'Carina? Are you all right?'

Slowly, Carina sat back and put a hand up to her head. 'Yes, I think so. I forgot to put the safety belt on. Oh!' She stared at the red stain on her fingers. 'It's blood.'

'What is it? What's happened?' Luis suddenly appeared beside them. 'Get out of the way, Stella. Let me get to her.' Opening the door, he put his arms round Carina and began to lift her out.

'No, it's nothing. Leave me alone!' She tried to push him away.

Luis swore under his breath in Portuguese, then said aloud, 'For once in your life, be sensible. Just keep still and let me help you.'

'I can manage. I can walk.'

But he swept her protests aside and picked her up in his arms, carrying her back to the villa, with Stella running anxiously alongside them.

Luis carried Carina into the sitting-room and set her down on the settee, then lifted her hair out of the way to look at her head, his hands infinitely gentle.

'Is it bad?' Stella asked worriedly.

'No, I don't think so. Go and get some warm water and cotton wool so that I can bathe it.' She ran to obey him, and Luis said roughly, 'You crazy little fool! You could have killed both yourself and Stella.'

'Do you think I don't know?' Carina answered in bitter self-reproach. 'I was—I was annoyed.'

'To say the least,' he agreed grimly. He was holding her head tilted a little to one side, his hand under her chin. Slowly, he ran his thumb over her mouth, his dark eyes fixed intently on her face. 'And all because I kissed you.'

'Because you forced yourself on me,' Carina corrected him coldly.

'You've changed,' he said softly. 'You used to love life, but now . . .' She opened her eyes fully and looked into his, waiting. 'But now you're so cold. It's as if your heart is frozen. I don't . . .'

But whatever he was going to say was lost, as Stella

came hurrying back and he began to bathe Carina's head.

'Shall I send for a doctor?' Stella asked, still anxious. 'Perhaps we should take her to a hospital.'

'I don't think it's that bad. Why don't you take over here while I get the car and drive it up to the house?'

'Yes, of course.' Stella knelt down beside her, as Luis left them together. 'Are you sure you're going to be all right, Carina? How do you feel?'

'Like a fool.' Sitting up, Carina firmly took the swab from Stella's hand and held it to her head. 'Stella, I'm dreadfully sorry. I was driving much too fast. I nearly hit you.'

'But you didn't. And you seem to have come off far worse. Why were you in such an all-fired hurry, for heaven's sake?'

'The usual reason,' Carina answered with a cynical smile. 'I'd just had a row with Luis. All I wanted to do was to get as far away from him as possible. It was a *driving* urge.'

Stella groaned. 'What a terrible pun. But at least it proves you're not badly hurt.'

'Of course I'm not. It was just a bump on the head.' Carina went to look at herself in a mirror on the wall, tilting her head to see the cut. It was about an inch long, just below her hairline on the left side of her head. 'I knew it was nothing to make a fuss about; all it needs is a plaster and I'll be as good as new.'

Luis came back into the room behind her and their eyes met in the mirror. There was a pinched look about his mouth and a bleak greyness in his eyes. Coming over to Carina, he put his hand lightly on her shoulder and turned her round. 'Yes, I think you're right. Stella, you'll find some dressings in the first-aid box in the kitchen.'

As soon as Stella went out of the room, Carina tried to duck from under his hand, but he held her still. 'When are you going to stop running away from me?' he said on a grim, soft note that somehow made it seem all the more bitter.

'Possibly when you stop behaving as if you own me. I'm not your possession, Luis. Even now, after all these years, you still think that I belong to you, that you can dictate to me. And you're still jealous—even though you have no right to be.'

'Hasn't every husband the right to be jealous of his wife?' Luis countered.

'Not when they've been separated for so long. Not when I've already offered you a divorce.'

'When we married, you vowed to be faithful to me. Till death.'

'Yes, I did,' Carina agreed, her voice rising in anger. 'And I promised to obey you, too, but I didn't know that also included having to obey your mother!'

'For heaven's sake!' Stella stood in the doorway, looking at them in amazement. 'Why on earth are you arguing about the past? It's over. Why don't you start again?' Coming across, she made Carina sit down while she put the plaster over her cut. 'How do you feel now?'

'Fine,' Carina lied, because her head had started to throb and her shoulder ached. 'Thanks for the first aid. I'll be getting along now.'

'You're not going anywhere.'

'Oh, no, you're not.'

Luis and Stella spoke together, then looked at each other and grinned.

'It seems that we're both in agreement,' Luis said. 'You can't possibly drive after that bump on the head. You should stay and rest, in case you have concussion.'

'Nonsense, I'm perfectly all right. I'll call in at your bar on Monday, Stell.'

She thought they would try to stop her again, and Stella did make a movement of protest, but Luis put out an arm and held her back.

The car was just outside the house again, with the keys still in it. Carina got in and remembered to put on her safety belt this time. Her hands were trembling a little, but for an entirely different reason than before; she didn't think she'd ever forget how close she'd come to killing Stella for as long as she lived. This time, she vowed, she would drive very, very slowly and carefully. She turned the key in the ignition, and the engine turned over but didn't fire. Twice more she tried, before she realised what must have happened.

Bristling with indignation, Carina walked through the house and found Luis and Stella on loungers by the pool. There was a third lounger now beside them. 'All right,' Carina said coldly. 'Whatever you did to the car, will you please go and put it right again?'

'Certainly,' Luis agreed. 'When we think you're well enough to drive.'

'Of all the high-handed ... If you don't fix it,' she threatened, 'I shall walk down to the main road and get a bus.'

'Nearly two miles, in this heat?' Luis looked at her disparagingly.

But Stella got to her feet and came over to take her arm. 'Please, darling, be sensible. Stay and have some lunch, and then see how you feel. You don't want to risk blacking out or something, and having a real accident, do you?'

Carina found herself cajoled into lying down on a lounger. A sunshade was put over her and a cold drink placed on a low table by her side. And although she wouldn't admit it, it was a relief to lie back and close her eyes, to try and shut out the throbbing in her head. Stella made a salad for lunch, but Carina didn't eat very much and soon lay back in the shade again, making no further attempt to try and leave. It would have been useless, anyway; there was a determined look about Luis's jawline that told her she was stuck here for the afternoon.

After a while, she fell asleep and woke feeling much better. The sun was still hot, but it was much lower in the sky, coruscating off the dappled waters of the pool as someone swam cleanly along its blue-tiled length. Carina sat up, putting up a hand to shield her eyes, so that she could see who it was. But the swimmer had seen her, and came quickly to the edge and heaved himself up and out of the pool. Luis walked over and stood looking down at her. His dark hair clung to his head, and beads of water ran down the long column of his neck, and on down to his slim athletic waist and flat stomach above the brief white bathing trunks that clung wetly to him, hiding none of his manhood.

Carina's throat tightened and she found it difficult to breathe. She had almost forgotten how beautiful his body was, his strong legs, the hard muscles in his arms and the width of his chest and shoulders. Her eyes shadowed as she ran the tip of her tongue along lips suddenly gone dry.

'That part was always good, wasn't it?'

She looked up and saw him smiling down at her, complete understanding in his eyes. 'Yes,' she admitted huskily. 'That was always good.'

Reaching down, Luis took her hand and helped her slowly to her feet. He stood for a long moment looking at her face, his eyes tender. 'Are you feeling better?'

'Yes. My head hardly aches at all now.'

'Good.' Lifting his hand, he gently stroked her hair back from her face, leaving little trails of moisture on her skin. The sun shone on his body, turning the drops of water into diamonds, so that he was clothed in them. Even the tiny drops on his eyelashes flashed iridescently. His fingers stroked her skin as lightly as a butterfly's wings, while his eyes held hers, making time seem to stand still. Then he slowly bent his head and touched her mouth with his. It wasn't a kiss—he asked and gave nothing—it was hardly more than a breath. And yet it moved Carina's heart far more than any kiss of passion and desire. She stood very still, almost afraid to breathe, until Luis drew back with a long sigh. 'You're so beautiful,' he murmured. 'So very lovely. How could I ever let you go?'

She shook her head, feeling tears pricking at her eyes. 'I loved you so much,' she said, in a voice so low it was less than a whisper.

'Carina?' He reached for her again, but she turned and began to walk towards the house.

'Where are you going?'

'I'm all right now. If you'll fix the car, I'll go.'

'Leaving won't help you to find out who Stella's boyfriend is. That *is* why you came here, isn't it?'

She paused and looked back. 'Yes, but I doubt if she'd

confide in me while you're here.' She gave a short laugh. 'Maybe she'll be more likely to confide in *you*.'

'Why don't you stay here with her?' Luis suggested, adding wryly, 'I'm only down for the weekend.'

'No, I couldn't do that.'

'Why not?'

'I should have thought it was obvious.'

'I've said I won't be here. And while you're my wife this is still your house, as is the house in Lisbon.'

Carina gave a rather bleak smile. 'I never felt as if I had a home with you. I always felt like a guest who'd more than outstayed her welcome.' Abruptly, she turned and walked to the edge of the terrace where there was an eye-dazzling view over the rolling, bushy landscape to the sea beyond. 'Why don't you come here any more?' she asked him.

'It has too many memories.'

She was silent for a moment, recalling how the house had evoked such poignant memories for her, too. Luis had come to stand beside her and she sneaked a look at him, but his head was turned away and she saw only his grim-mouthed profile. 'Yes,' she said stiltedly, 'I suppose coming here would awaken unhappy memories.'

Luis turned to face her. 'You're mistaken. I meant happy ones. Memories so happy that I just can't bear to relive them.'

That the house should have the same effect on them both took her aback, and it was several seconds before Carina could say, 'I—I'm glad.'

'Glad?' Luis raised his eyebrows in self-mockery. 'That I went through hell after you left?'

'No. That . . .' Carina bit her lip for a moment. 'That

there were some happy times for you to remember.'

He made a half-movement towards her, but then stopped short and said masochistically, 'Are you saying that you've forgotten them?'

She turned away. 'I try never to think about our marriage. It's over. It's in the past,' she said firmly. 'I think only about the present and the future.'

'And is Greg Summers part of your future?' Luis demanded tersely, suddenly angry again.

'He may be,' Carina returned, looking at him over her shoulder. 'But whether he is or not is nothing to do with you; I've told you that before.'

Luis was silent for a moment until, his voice grating, he said bitterly, 'I suppose there have been many men in your life since you left me?'

Carina turned to face him fully, anger rising, but as she looked into Luis's face and saw the bleakness and hurt in his eyes, the rigid set of his jaw as he strove to control himself, her heart was moved and anger died. It was obvious now that her leaving him had hurt him far more than she had ever realised. But when she'd left Portugal and he had refused to make his home in England as she'd demanded, her thoughts and emotions had all been centred on herself, not on what Luis had been going through at all. She had felt so neglected and betrayed—emotions fostered and encouraged by her own mother—and bitterly angry that Luis wouldn't relent and do as she wanted. At the time, she had felt convinced that he didn't love her enough to give up the home and family that she had grown to detest, and start a new life with her in England. When he'd come after her to take her back to Portugal, Carina had given him an ultimatum: Portugal or me. He had told her not to be such a little fool and ordered her to go back with him. And she had refused, point blank. Luis, his pride hurt, had tried to force her instead of persuading her, but she had resisted him and her mother had intervened.

Carina could remember him now, his face white with fury, saying hotly, 'When you come to your senses—or grow up enough to leave your mother's apron-strings—then you can send for me and I'll come for you.' But she had never sent for him, although she had seen through her mother soon enough. She had pride, too, and it had been hurt just as much as his.

Abruptly dragging her thoughts back to the present, she said, 'Yes, there have been other men. But none of them meant anything.'

'And am I supposed to take comfort from that?' Luis demanded harshly.

'You can take it how you damn well like!' Carina retorted, angry again, because she *had* said it to comfort him. 'I couldn't care less.'

Leaving him on the terrace, Carina walked into the house to look for Stella, and found her in the kitchen. 'Do something for me, will you?' she said to the younger girl. 'Persuade Luis to fix my car so that I can leave.'

'Sorry,' Stella returned cheerfully. 'Can't you see that I'm in the process of cooking us all a meal? It's one of my specials; sweet and sour pork, and egg and shrimp fried rice. Oh, and there are some barbecued ribs, too.'

'Chinese food? In Portugal?'

'Why not? I thought Luis might be tired of eating Portuguese and would like a change.'

'You're very fond of him, aren't you?' Carina asked, with a little catch in her voice.

'Yes, I suppose I am. I thought it was marvellous when you married him. He was so gorgeously masculine and good-looking. And I thought I was going to get the big brother I had always wanted.' She gave Carina a sidelong look as she stirred the contents of a frying-pan. 'You didn't think that I was gone on him or anything, did you?'

'I thought you might have a schoolgirl crush, yes.'

'Oh, I *did*—when I was a schoolgirl.'

'And now?'

'And now—I suppose I like him as a friend, and just wish you two hadn't split up. As for myself, I have other interests.'

Tired of playing games, Carina came right out and said, 'Just who is your boyfriend, Stell?'

'Are you going to stay to dinner?'

'No, I told you, I'm going back to my hotel. Stella, for heaven's sake, I . . .'

'I only asked,' Stella interrupted smoothly, 'because I would have introduced you to him. But as you're determined not to stay . . .'

'You mean, you've invited this man to dinner?' Carina exclaimed in astonishment.

'That's right. He should be here any time now.'

'Does Luis know?'

Stella shook her head while juggling with the frying-pan and a bowl. 'No, I forgot to tell him. Pass me that cloth, would you?'

Carina did so, and gave her an indignant glare. 'You *knew* I didn't want to stay.'

'Nobody's making you,' Stella laughed. 'But somehow I don't think you're going to be able to resist staying to meet Kurt.'

'Kurt? That can't be a Portuguese name.'

'So who said he was Portuguese? *I* certainly didn't.'

'Stella, I could brain you! And you needn't think I don't know what you're up to; you're trying to get Luis and I back together. Well, it won't work!'

'So what are you getting so worked up about, then?'

'I'm not, I . . .' Carina broke off and sighed. 'I can't have dinner in just shorts and a suntop,' she said, capitulating. 'Can I borrow something of yours?'

'Help yourself. Dinner will be ready in half an hour. Will you tell Luis?'

Going along the corridor, Carina rapped on Luis's door.

'Who is it?'

'Carina.'

'Come in.'

But he was using their old room, and she didn't want to be in there with him again. She began to call out to him, but her voice died as Luis pulled the door open. He was wearing a dark blue towelling robe with his initials embroidered on the pocket, the one she had given him for the one and only Christmas they had been together. One of their few happy times that they had spent here in the villa, alone, but only for a couple of days before they were summoned back to Lisbon, by his father who supposedly needed Luis on a lawsuit. But Carina had been quite sure that his mother had been behind it.

'I came to tell you that Stella is cooking dinner for us. She says it will be ready in half an hour. And she's invited her boyfriend.'

Luis's eyebrows rose. 'So we're going to find out who he is at last. You are staying, of course?'

'Yes. I'm going to borrow something of Stella's to wear.'

'Would you like to change in here?'

'No.' She said it too fast and too vehemently, and Luis's eyes went to her face intently. Trying to sound calm, Carina said, 'Thanks, but I might as well use Stella's room.' She nodded. 'See you later.' She then walked along to the other room, but was aware that Luis watched her the whole way. At the door, she was unable to resist turning to look at him. Their eyes met, but she quickly lowered her glance and went inside.

Carina chose an Indian cotton dress in a deep wine colour, with threads of silver running through it. The dress had long sleeves, tiny buttons down the bodice, and a full, long skirt. She showered and changed into it, adding a pair of Stella's silver sandals and helping herself to make-up and perfume. When she was nearly ready, Stella came flying in to check her hair and add the finishing touches to her own appearance.

'Hey, you look great in that!' she exclaimed generously. 'Much better than I do. I bought it in Lisbon, and I've only worn it a couple of . . .' The front doorbell rang and she gave an exclamation of annoyance. 'Oh, damn, that must be Kurt! Do I look all right?' she asked anxiously, pulling a comb through her thick fair hair.

'Yes, fine. Stella,' Carina put out a hand to stop her as she turned to hurry away. 'Is he very special, this Kurt?'

Stella looked back at her speculatively. 'Why? Are you starting to feel sympathetic?'

Releasing her arm, Carina drew back. 'I just don't want you to get hurt, that's all.'

With a laugh, Stella answered, 'Oh, don't worry, Sis; I'm quite capable of handling my own life—even if you weren't.' And she ran to eagerly let her boyfriend in.

Carina heard their voices, but didn't hurry to meet Kurt, instead, taking an unnecessarily long time to finish getting ready. Somehow she felt strangely reluctant to see the two of them together. Because she might see in their faces the love and hope for the future that had once been in hers and Luis's? she wondered as she looked at her own reflection in the mirror. Love, she'd decided a long time go, was cruel; it lifted you to the peak of happiness and expectancy, only to send you hurtling back to the ground, crying out in pain at the hurt. A hurt that even now was still sometimes raw and bleeding, making her shrink from ever trusting her emotions again.

Only when Carina heard Luis go down the corridor, and his voice joined with the others, did she come out to join them. They were all in the kitchen, and she could hear Stella laughingly telling the men to get out of her way or dinner would never be ready. Carina paused for a moment in the doorway leading from the kitchen to the dining-room, and took a good look at Kurt. He was entirely different from what she'd expected. He wasn't tall, or particularly handsome or dashing. He was of medium height and rather stocky, with light brown hair and a pleasant, open face. He looked kind and intelligent and dependable. And Carina's heart sank. This was the type of man a girl *ought* to marry. The kind you could love whole-heartedly, if unexcitingly, all your life and be utterly content. He wasn't the kind of man you fell head over heels in love with at first sight, and out again just as easily, and so was infinitely more dangerous. If Stella was beginning to love him, then it would be next to impossible to make her give him up.

Luis glanced up and saw her, his mouth twisting in amusement when he saw the dismay in her eyes. Going over to her, he put a determined hand under Carina's elbow and drew her forward to join them. 'This is Stella's sister, Carina,' he introduced her, adding mendaciously, 'My wife. And this, darling, is Kurt van Dyckel. He's Dutch,' he added unnecessarily.

They exchanged greetings, Kurt giving a little bow as he shook her hand. He spoke English very well, although not as well as Luis. But then, Luis had had plenty of practice.

'Dinner in five minutes,' Stella sang out. 'You've just got time to have a quick drink. And will you *please* have it in the sitting-room, not in the kitchen? I can't move!'

Luis laughed. 'I think the cook is getting a little tense.' He led the way out of the room, planting a friendly kiss on Stella's bare shoulders as he passed. Carina immediately looked to see how Kurt would take this, but he was smiling and didn't seem to mind at all.

While Luis got her a drink, Carina asked Kurt if he was living in Portugal.

'Oh, yes. I am here as a courier with a travel company, but I shall take up a position as an accountant when I return home.'

'You're here for the whole summer, then?'

'Yes, until October, at least.'

Carina's heart sank again and it didn't help any to see the open laughter in Luis's eyes. Coming over to her, he handed her a drink and slipped an arm round her waist. 'You look very lovely, darling,' he said caressingly.

She glared at him under her lashes and tried to move away, but he held her firmly by his side, his arm strong as steel.

'Your villa is very beautiful,' Kurt complimented, looking at Carina. 'Do you live here all the time?'

'No, I don't . . .'

But Luis broke in quickly with, 'I have a law practice in Lisbon, so this is only a holiday home.'

Stella's announcement that dinner was ready saved Luis from having to make any more explanations, much to Carina's annoyance. It was silly to pretend that things were other than what they were, especially to a comparative stranger like Kurt. What did it matter if he knew the truth? Stella had probably told him what the situation was, anyway.

Stella had set the table with candles and a central bowl of hibiscus blooms from the garden. She had so obviously gone to a lot of trouble over the meal that Carina determined that it should be a happy one for her. Putting aside her fears about Kurt, and her annoyance with Luis, she joined in the conversation readily, often laughing, her dry wit adding sparkle to the evening. Luis sat next to her, on her right, and Kurt on her left. Stella wouldn't let her help with the dishes at the end of the meal, but Kurt insisted, which left Luis and Carina alone at the table, sipping their brandy.

'It's a long time since we had a meal together,' he remarked reflectively. 'Even with other people.'

'Yes, but we seldom ate alone, anyway,' Carina pointed out. 'When we were in Lisbon, we always had to eat with your parents or else go out to a restaurant.'

'Did you hate living with my parents so much?'

'Yes, I did.'

His dark eyes studied her intently. 'You never said so—not until you were back in England.'

'I asked you to find us somewhere to live, somewhere where there would be just the two of us. But you didn't take me seriously. You just kept putting me off.'

'If I remember correctly, I was very busy at the time.

My father had given me some important cases to deal with and I ...'

'Yes, I know,' Carina broke in. 'Which is why I didn't push it, why I tried not to give you an extra worry by letting you see how unhappy I was.' She gave a brittle smile. 'But I see now that that was a mistake. Maybe if you'd realised how hard your mother was trying to get rid of me, you might have done something about it.'

Luis stared at her. 'Are you accusing my mother of deliberately trying to split us up?'

Carina gave him back stare for stare. 'No, I'm accusing her of *succeeding*. Oh, Luis, how could you have been so *blind*?'

'You said something like this when I went to England to bring you back, but I thought it was something that your own mother had put into your head. You seemed happy enough.'

'You saw only what you wanted to see,' she said passionately, but then paused. 'No, that isn't fair. I was *happy* when I was with you. But when you were working, all the week and so often late at night, then I was alone with your mother and she made my life hell.'

'Why didn't you tell me?'

She gave him an angry look. 'Because I was in love with you. Because I didn't want to come between you and your mother. Because I hoped and prayed that you'd see for yourself, and take me away from there. Because you were so terribly busy and I wanted to shield you from ...'

His hand shot out and covered hers as it lay on the table, silencing her. His eyes, hard and cold, were intent on her face. 'You were *shielding* me?'

Shaking off his hand, Carina stood up. 'Oh, what does it matter now?'

'It *does* matter.' Luis, too, got to his feet. 'Why didn't you tell me all this before?'

'I tried! That last time. But you were—I suppose we were *both* too emotional to even communicate rationally. You were so hell bent on making me go back to you. And I knew that I just couldn't stand living in the same house as your parents again. It was all so hopeless.' She shook her head in remembered despair.

'We could have worked it out,' Luis said roughly.

'You mean, if we'd loved each other enough we might have. But we didn't—that became all too painfully obvious.' Suddenly tired of raking up the past, Carina said, 'I don't want to talk about it any more. My head aches and I want to go home.'

Luis looked at her drawn face and was about to say something, but Stella and Kurt came back into the room.

'We've had the most marvellous idea!' Stella exclaimed. 'Why don't we all spend the day together tomorrow? We could go out on Luis's boat and have a barbecue on a beach somewhere. One of those you can only reach by sea. You'd like that, wouldn't you, Carina?' she urged enthusiastically.

'What about Kurt's job?' Carina temporised.

'Tomorrow is my day off,' the Dutch boy told her.

'It sounds a great idea,' Luis agreed. 'And it will give us all a chance to get to know Kurt better,' he added for Carina's benefit.

'Marvellous. You will come with us, won't you, Sis?' Stella pleaded.

Caught between inclination and her promise to her

mother, Carina said, 'Well, I suppose I could, but . . .'

'Good, that's settled, then,' Luis cut in adroitly. 'We'll make an early start, shall we? Can you manage that, Kurt?'

'Of course he can,' Stella answered for him. 'He can stay here tonight, can't he, Luis?'

'Of course. You're most welcome, Kurt.'

Carina knew exactly what was coming next, and gave both Luis and Stella a fulminating glance. 'Do you know, I somehow get the feeling that I'm being manipulated,' she said icily.

Stella laughed and came over to hug her. 'Of course you are. So why don't you relax and enjoy yourself?'

'I shall have words with you later,' Carina warned threateningly. But it was impossible to be mad with Stella when she was in such a happy mood.

They sat and talked over another drink, Carina slipping off her sandals so that she could tuck her feet under her in the armchair. She watched Stella and Kurt covertly, looking for any telltale signs of love. Stella seemed happy enough, as did Kurt, but neither of them showed any signs of being gone on each other. Of the two of them, it was Kurt who picked up Stella's hand and held it as they sat on the couch, only for her to pluck it away when next she spoke and made some gesture. And the admiring looks he gave her weren't returned at all.

'Where did you two meet?' Carina asked curiously.

'At the bar where I work. Kurt stopped for a drink there one day and we got talking.'

'So you haven't known each other long, then?'

'Oh, long enough. Haven't we, Kurt?' Stella squeezed his hand and gave him such a dazzling smile that Kurt could only nod in happy bemusement.

Carina's eyes narrowed; she was almost sure now that

the postcards Stella had sent her mother had been a ruse to make her come here. She must have known that their mother would be worried and would get Carina to go to Portugal, and she had also known that at some point Carina and Luis would be bound to meet. Carina wouldn't have put it past her sister to have sent for Luis if Carina had bypassed him and gone straight to the villa in search of her. She had suspected as much before, but the arrival of Kurt on the scene had temporarily thrown her. Seeing them together, though, Carina began to believe that he, too, was just part of Stella's elaborate trick to try to get she and Luis back together.

Carina sipped her drink, and looked at Stella thoughtfully, wondering why she had gone to such lengths. She must have known that the marriage was dead, so why put them through these emotional traumas for no reason?

Glancing across at Luis, Carina saw an amused light in his eyes as he watched her. Damn him, she thought angrily, he knows exactly what I'm thinking. And he knows that I'm right, too. Her eyes frowned as it occurred to her that Luis might have known all along. But she swiftly dismissed the idea. He certainly hadn't at first—no one could have faked the emotions he'd shown when she surprised him at his office. But had he seen through the deception and gone along with it since? But if so—why? Her heart began to beat a little faster, and she pushed the thought out of her mind. It was a crazy idea. Quite impossible. If Luis wanted her back, why hadn't he bothered to get in touch with her during the long years they'd been separated? Looking at Kurt and Stella again, Carina decided that she would watch them tomorrow, and if she was sure that it was all a deception and Stella was in no danger of emulating her own mistake, then she would go home at once. She didn't like being used, and she certainly had no part in this charade.

Finishing her drink, she stood up. 'I'm tired. I'll see you all in the morning. Goodnight.'

Luis followed her out of the room and she gave him a suspicious look. 'What do you want?'

'Merely to see that you're comfortable. You'll take the master bedroom, of course?'

'No, thanks. The other guest room will be fine.'

Luis raised a sardonic eyebrow. 'Isn't that taking your dislike of my parents to extreme lengths?'

'Probably,' she agreed. 'But I don't intend to try to sleep in their bed.'

His mouth thinned, but he said, 'As you wish,' and followed her to the other guest room. 'It looks as if Stella has already made the bed up.'

'That doesn't surprise me in the least,' Carina said drily.

'You think she made it up for Kurt?'

'No, I don't. And I don't think you're that obtuse, either. Stella wants me to stay.'

'You're her sister, of course she wants you to stay with her. Perhaps she's beginning to get lonely, travelling around Europe on her own.'

Carina laughed at the thought. 'I very much doubt that. Stella is the type of girl who makes friends wherever she goes. And she's right; she can handle her life far better than I ever could. I should have remembered that before I came hurrying over here, on what I strongly suspect will turn out to be a wild-goose chase.'

'But you thought she might need you, so you came.

Isn't that all that matters?'

'Possibly.' She glanced up at him and was suddenly aware of him as a man, of his size and strength, of remembered nights held in his arms, nights of erotic passion and love. He somehow made the room seem much smaller, and she felt dwarfed by him. Her voice tight in her throat, Carina said, 'If you'll excuse me, I'd like to go to bed now.'

'Are you sending me away to play blackberry to Stella and Kurt?'

'I think you mean gooseberry. Your English is slipping.'

'It's a long time since I had private lessons,' Luis reminded her, his voice low and insinuating. 'Couldn't I stay so that we could talk?'

'No!' The word came out violently. 'I've had enough. Just go away, Luis, and leave me alone.'

His face hardening, he said with cold courtesy, 'Of course. I beg your pardon. Goodnight, Carina.'

Despite her tiredness, Carina found it difficult to sleep. So much had happened today. Seeing Luis had been a shock, and having to spend most of the day in close proximity to him had been quite a strain. So many memories had come back; good ones, bad ones. Carina tried to push them out of her mind, but they wouldn't go away. Outside she heard the others taking a midnight swim, laughing and splashing, but trying to keep their voices hushed so they wouldn't wake her. And then there were only two voices, just Kurt's and Stella's. Carina could imagine Luis going back to his room to dry off, and rubbing the big towel over his tall, athletic body, a task that on their honeymoon she had often done for him, lingeringly, until she wasn't rubbing any more,

Luis was standing up by the mast, showing Stella which ropes operated the sails. He was wearing only a pair of shorts, and his body looked lean and brown as he stood close to Stella in her minute bikini. For a moment Carina felt a stab of jealousy—not for her sister, but for the girl she herself had once been, who had stood exactly like that with Luis aeons of time ago. Luis must have felt her eyes on him, for he turned to face her and in her heightened perceptivity she saw that he understood, and in teaching Stella he, too, was reliving those far-off days.

After she'd put the sails up and down a couple of times and had a go at the tiller, Stella came over to sit beside Carina. 'That was fun! Phew, it's hot already. Will you put some oil on my back for me?'

'Don't you want Kurt to do it?' Carina asked mockingly, as she unscrewed the bottle.

Stella grinned. 'It's too early in the day. You're very quiet this morning. You haven't still got a headache, have you?'

'No, I'm fine. Just—reflective.'

'Being here is bringing it all back, is it?' Stella asked, unable to completely hide the note of satisfaction in her voice.

'Isn't that what you intended?'

'Me? I didn't intend anything,' the younger girl declared innocently.

'Liar. I've known you too many years to be fooled for long.' She rubbed in the oil down to Stella's bikini line. 'There, you should fry nicely now.' But before she moved away Carina said on a warning note, 'I know you have the best of intentions, Stella, but just remember what happened last time; I ran away from Luis, then. Bringing it all back may make me run away again—and for good this time.'

A shadow crossed Stella's face. She nodded, but two minutes later was laughing happily with Kurt.

They sailed to a beach that could be reached only by sea, the high sandstone cliffs, pock-marked by caves, rising high into the sky around it. There were no other boats there, and they expected to have the place to themselves, but as they went nearer in they saw that there were already two lots of people settled on the sands.

'I'm afraid we're going to find this whichever beach we go to,' Luis remarked. 'The boat operators in the tourist towns have got wise to it and operate a taxi service, bringing people out here in the morning and picking them up in the evening. What do you say—shall we stay here or try to find somewhere else?'

'Oh, let's stay,' Stella decided. 'We'll still have lots of space to ourselves.'

So Luis dropped anchor, and they rowed the picnic ashore in the rubber dinghy, Kurt swimming alongside because there wasn't enough room for him. After staking their claim to a part of the beach with towels and an umbrella, they swam and played *pétanque* for an hour before having their lunch. They drank wine and laughed and talked a lot, Carina having to keep reminding herself that she was only there to watch Kurt and Stella. It was all too easy to fall into the trap set by the sun and the holiday mood, and impossible to be aloof. Not that Stella would have allowed her to be, anyway. But, luckily, Luis seemed to be in a carefree mood, too, so that she could relax and join in the fun.

Or he was until they settled down after lunch to rest and sunbathe. Stella unhooked her bikini top without a moment's thought, and it was quite obvious that she had

done so before with Kurt because he didn't turn a hair.
Luis glanced at her and then looked at Carina with an
amused half-smile, quite confident that she wouldn't
follow suit. Portuguese men, Carina knew, still had a
slight primitive streak of jealousy where their women
were concerned, and the only time she had taken her top
off when she was living in Portugal was when she and
Luis had been completely alone together on a beach,
usually the private one below the villa, or one like this.
On a public beach she had always kept decorously
covered, knowing he didn't altogether approve. But
now, in a moment of bravado, Carina took off her bikini
top as casually as Stella had done and dropped it on to the
sand beside her. Kurt gave her an admiring glance, but
Luis's face hardened, the smile disappearing. Carina
met his look challengingly, her eyes telling him that she
didn't belong to him any more and she'd do what she
damn well liked.

She lay back and closed her eyes, soaking up the sun,
and felt Luis lie down beside her, but she made no
attempt to speak to him and soon fell asleep.

Fingers were gently stroking her arm, the touch warm
and familiar. Carina gave a little sigh of contentment and
moved towards the hand, which tightened on her arm.
Then she remembered where she was, and her eyes
blinked open. Luis was lying on his side, propped up on
his elbow, his eyes dark as he went on stroking her.

'The sun's gone round,' he said softly. 'I don't want
you to get burnt.'

'Where are the others?' Carina asked, as she sat up
and saw they were alone.

'Swimming.' He gestured towards the sea. 'Would
you like me to put some oil on for you?'

She gave a small smile. 'No, thanks.'

'You'd rather get burnt than have me touch you, is that it?' Luis demanded, creating an immediate tension between them.

'Haven't you heard?' Carina responded tartly. 'You only get burnt if you play with fire. I did once, and I certainly don't intend to again.' Getting to her feet with a graceful movement, she said, 'I think I'll go and have a swim to cool off.'

She ran down to the water and plunged in, joining Stella and Kurt, but Luis stayed on the beach, watching. They swam for about half an hour, but when they came out the sun was blazingly hot and the only shade was that given by the umbrella. Luis was more or less impervious to the sun, his skin already so darkly tanned that he wouldn't burn, but the others all had much fairer skins, and Carina, especially, couldn't take too much. 'This is too much for me,' Stella declared. 'Why don't we go back to the boat and go on somewhere else?'

'That's fine by me.' Carina picked up her towel, but there was no need to dry herself, the sun had aready done that for her.

Back on the boat, Luis sailed further along the coastline and once took them right inside a huge cave in the cliffs. As the boat entered, the sun was suddenly blotted out and it seemed very cold. Looking up above the top of the mast with its gay pennant, Carina saw millions of seashells compacted into the rock, holding the sandstone together. The sheer weight of the cliff above them seemed to press down on her, making her feel small and vulnerable. Kurt and Stella had been calling out to create an echo, but they, too, seemed to feel the oppressiveness of the place and fell silent.

Carina shivered. 'Let's go back. It's like a tomb.'

It was both a relief and a pleasure to get back in the sun again. This time they sailed to a big public beach, the sand almost lost beneath the shades and umbrellas. The beach had a café with a shady awning, the supplies for the place sent down from the top of the cliff in a basket attached to a rope, to save carrying them down the steep flights of steps. The café's speciality was barbecued sardines; the fish—large by English standards—caught in the sea and cooked fresh every day. They were served with a big plateful of green salad and chunks of crusty bread—and chips if you were English and just had to have chips with everything.

The four of them decided against the chips, but tucked into the sardines, hungry again even after their picnic, and thirsty for a cool beer. Carina picked delicately at the silver fish, trying to remove all the bones. Luis watched her and then laughed. 'You never did know how to dissect a sardine.'

Looking at the mess she was making of the job, Carina laughed too, suddenly feeling young and happy again.

Luis's dark eyes rested on her face, his own smiling back. 'Such a small thing,' he said for only her to hear. 'To make you laugh *with* me at last.'

Taking the plate from her, he began to fillet the fish neatly and efficiently. Carina watched him for a moment, and then said in a low voice, 'Have I been so—disagreeable?'

'Not disagreeable, no. Just cold and withdrawn. I was beginning to be afraid that you had lost all your warmth.' His eyes met hers. 'That I had killed it.'

She stared at him but, before she could think of anything to say, Stella and Kurt had finished their own conversation, so they started talking about something else.

After they'd eaten, Luis hired one of the big shades on the beach, and they all sat under it, Carina trying to read a novel in Portuguese that she'd found at the villa. All the books in English that she'd left there had disappeared; thrown away, she supposed wryly, by Luis's mother. But she was very conscious of Luis lounging beside her, and found it difficult to concentrate. Every few minutes, Carina would lift her head and look around, watching the other people on the beach, but not really aware of them.

'Dare you to swim round the island,' Stella said to Kurt, and the two of them ran off to try to go round a large, high rock, once part of the eroded cliffs, that stuck up out of the middle of the bay.

Carina watched them go, giving up the attempt to read her book. 'Is it dangerous?' she asked a trifle anxiously.

'No, they're both good swimmers, and there are plenty of pedaloes and canoes out there to help them if they get in difficulties.'

'I suppose so.' She watched them for a while, until she was sure the swim was within their capabilities, then looked round the beach again. There was so much going on, a constant movement of people, but one group who were comparatively still caught her eye. From their complexions and the decorous swimsuits that the women wore, Carina guessed they were Portuguese. They were standing in a largish group, but talking among themselves, which the Portuguese tended to do. Two women on the outskirts of the group were having a very earnest conversation with a lot of gesticulating, but one of them was holding the hand of a tiny little girl, probably not more than two or three years old. The child stood docilely by her mother, a bucket and spade in her other hand. To protect her head from the sun she wore a blue sunhat, but otherwise was completely naked, her little behind as brown as the rest of her skin.

When Carina saw the child, her lips curved into a smile, but then her face grew sad and wistful.

'It could have been our child,' Luis said deliberately.

She turned, realising that he had been watching her. For a moment, anguish filled her heart as Carina thought that she might never have a child, would certainly never have Luis's. Taking refuge in mockery to hide her feelings, she said flippantly, 'No, it couldn't. Your mother would never have allowed a Riveiro to go naked on the beach—even one as young as that.'

But Luis wasn't to be put off so easily. Picking up her hand, he said, 'You know, I don't believe you're as hard as you make out. I'm definitely beginning to see cracks in that wall you've built around yourself.'

Carina shrugged. 'People change as they get older. I'm not as naïve as I was, that's all.'

'Don't you ever wish that we'd had a child?'

'Certainly not,' Carina answered firmly. 'It would only have complicated matters. Even your mother advised me against starting a family.'

His eyes came swiftly up to her face. 'You never told me that.' His jaw hardened. 'Did you decide to "shield" me from that, too?'

'What would have been the point in telling you?'

Suddenly forceful, Luis said, 'Did it ever occur to you that by withholding all the things that were making you unhappy, you were denying me the right to protect and shield *you*? I thought you were happy. You always gave that impression. I thought the only thing at all wrong between us was that I was having to work such long hours, and we couldn't see as much of each other as we would have liked. But I thought that, once that period was over, everything would be all right and we would have plenty of time together again.' His voice shook. 'It came as the most terrible, unbelievable shock when you went to visit your mother and wrote and said you weren't coming back.'

'Look, it's over. I . . .'

'No!' His grip tightened, hurting her. 'We must talk this out. As—as calmly and rationally as we can. I went through hell after you left, thinking that you didn't love me enough, or that I'd failed you in some way—but I didn't know how. I hoped against hope that you would miss me and want to come back. That's why I wrote to Stella secretly. If she had given me the slightest hint that you had wanted to go on with the marriage, I would have gone straight over again for you.' His face darkened. 'But then she told me that you had started going out with other men,' he said bitterly.

Carina sat silently, marvelling that she had managed to hide her feelings so well. Right from the time she'd left him, she had missed Luis dreadfully, and when he didn't write or phone she had only gone out on dates to try and take her mind off him, to try to hide her aching heart. But that period in her life hadn't lasted very long. She had soon realised that there was no one who could take Luis's place in her heart, and that to go on looking in this desperate kind of way would only lead to even more unhappiness. And it was then that she'd left her home and got herself a flat, away from her mother's incessant urgings for her to get a divorce.

With a sigh, Carina said, 'Yes, I went on dates. But that's all they were, nothing more. It wasn't—like the way you make it sound. I was just trying to get my self-confidence back, that was all. But it didn't work.' Musingly she said, 'I find that self-confidence is exactly what it says; the assurance has to come from within yourself. Other people can't give it to you, not really. Oh, they can boost your morale and make you feel good, especially someone you love, but when they leave you, then you plummet right down again. Having real *self*-confidence is believing in yourself without other people—or even despite them,' she finished wryly.

'Yes,' Luis agreed, 'I suppose that's the change I've seen in you. You're independent now, and you weren't entirely before.'

'No, I was dependent on you.' Carina paused deliberately. 'But you let me down.'

'Not knowingly,' Luis put in swiftly.

She looked into his face. 'But that's just the point, isn't it? You should have known.'

He looked at her for a long moment, before turning away and saying heavily, 'Yes, you're right. I suppose you saying that you wanted a place of our own should have told me there was something seriously wrong, but I thought you were just being—English.'

'English?' Carina gave him a startled look. 'Oh, you mean that young Portuguese couples are more willing to accept living with their in-laws? Actually, I wouldn't have minded too much, but it was my Englishness that your mother couldn't take. I think your father quite liked me, but he had to follow your mother's lead.'

They both fell silent, thinking about those few

months they'd been together, until Luis broke the silence by saying, 'You said that the men you dated didn't mean anything, but what about this man you were in Lisbon with, Greg Summers—does he mean anything?'

Carina stood up and looked towards the sea, shading her eyes. 'They've gone round the rock. Look, they've stopped to talk to those people in the yellow pedalo.'

Luis got to his feet and walked round in front of her, blocking out the sun. 'You haven't answered my question,' he said tersely.

'What makes you think I'm going to answer it? It's too late to start being jealous, Luis. Much too late. What I do in my life is my own affair now. Not yours, my mother's, or anyone else's.'

'That makes it sound as if he isn't important,' Luis persisted.

'Oh, for heaven's sake! He may become important— he may not. I don't know! Now just leave it, will you? I can't understand why you keep asking all these questions, anyway.'

'Can't you?' Reaching forward Luis put his hands on her bare waist. 'Because I want you back, of course. Because I want us to be husband and wife again.' His hands tightened as his voice became intense. 'We were happy once, we can be again. I know it. We're both older and wiser, so we won't make the same mistakes. We won't ...'

'My God, you've got a nerve!' Carina knocked his hands away. 'All those years of silence, and then we see each other for just a few days and you turn round and say you want me back. Just like that! Of all the arrogant, conceited ...' For a moment, words failed her, but then she said venomously, 'Has it ever occurred to you, Luis, that I might not want *you* back? That I might like the life I'm leading now, like being free and independent? I'm my own mistress now—not yours or any other man's,' she said derisively. 'You've no need to be jealous of any other man, because I have something far more precious—freedom. And I don't intend to give it up.'

'And love?' Luis demanded tersely. 'Can you live without that?'

'Love?' Carina gave a high-pitched laugh of derision, which made several people look round at them. 'That's just a word. A figment of the imagination. All there is is basic physical chemistry. It either lasts or it doesn't. And with us it didn't.'

'No?' Luis grabbed at her arm. 'Are you so sure of that?' he questioned fiercely.

'Yes, I am.' She looked up at him tauntingly and then down at his hand holding her wrist. 'What do you intend to do—throw me down on to the sand here and now?'

Slowly, Luis let go of her, his eyes flashing angry fire. 'No, not here and now,' he answered menacingly. 'But one day soon I'm going to prove to you just how wrong you are.'

An uncertain look came into Carina's green eyes, but she gave a disbelieving laugh of mockery. 'You don't really think I'm going to fall for that line, do you? It doesn't impress me a bit, if that's what you're trying to do.'

A cold look came into Luis's face. 'No, I'm not trying to impress you, I'm just trying to make you stop being so defensive. To look inside your own heart. You may have become more independent, Carina, but I don't believe that you've changed inside. I won't believe it. You're basically the same girl that I met and fell in love with.'

Carina shook her head. 'You're wrong. That person
doesn't exist any more—and I'm glad she doesn't,' she
added, so softly that Luis only just heard.

Turning away, Carina walked down to the water's
edge to look for Stella and Kurt. She stood with her feet
in the shallows, looking over the sun-dappled sea. When
she saw them still swimming in the water, she waved,
but didn't go back to Luis. Her heart was beating too
loudly, it seemed to fill her chest. Her emotions were a
shattered mixture of anger, amazement, scorn and
disbelief, with somewhere deep in her heart a tiny note
of longing.

She had known that the physical attraction was still
there for Luis, of course. Otherwise, he would never
have kissed her as he had yesterday, with a kind of savage
passion over which he had little or no control. But she
had thought he'd done so out of hurt pride, and that he
needed to prove to himself that he could still take her
whenever he wanted her, that she was still as unable to
resist him as before. But that he should want to get back
together, to try again; that had certainly never occurred
to her. She understood now why he had been so eager to
discuss the past and find out exactly what had gone
wrong. But that he should come right out and suggest
living together again—the whole idea was ridiculous!

Carina told herself this several times as she stood in
the sunlight, the water lapping at her toes; but, no
matter how many times, there was still a warm feeling in
her heart that he cared, that he had never entirely
stopped loving her. Not that she intended to take any
notice of that feeling, of course, she was much too
sensible ever to be ruled by her emotions again—but it

didn't do that self-confidence, of which she was so proud, any harm at all to know that Luis still wanted her.

As if drawn by some compulsion, Carina turned and looked back at where they had been sitting. Luis was standing half-in and half-out of the shadow, his arm leaning on one of the awning supports. His head and the upper part of his body was in the sunlight, his waist and legs in the shade, so that as she turned, half dazzled by the sun, for a brief instant he appeared to be naked. Carina gasped, the memory of his body holding her, loving her, filling her with ecstatic joy, flooded through her veins, making her feel suddenly giddy. She reeled and stumbled a little, dropping to her knees in the tiny rippling waves.

Immediately, Luis ran across and stood over her. He seemed so tall, so like a giant in his strength and masculinity as she looked up at him. Her lips parted, but were so dry that she couldn't speak, could only gaze upwards, her eyes wide with a mixture of awe and fear. Reaching down, Luis held out his hands to her. Slowly, she put hers in them and he used the strength in his arms to draw her to her feet, her body sliding along the length of his as he slowly lifted her. His hands tightened as he looked into her face intently, and Carina knew that if they had been alone he would have kissed her again. And right now she wasn't at all sure that she could have resisted him.

'You see,' Luis said in low pleasure. 'You want me as much as I want you.'

'No, it wasn't that. I—the sun—I turned my head too quickly and my eyes couldn't adjust. It made me feel giddy.' But she spoke too fast and too protestingly to convince him.

'I don't believe you.' Still holding her hand, he drew her beside him into deeper water. The coolness of it reached her knees, then her hips, but still Luis led her farther out, until the sea came above her shoulders. His eyes held hers as they waded in, and his grip was firm, ready to resist any effort she might make to break free.

He stopped and turned to face her. Letting go of her hand, he put both of his on her shoulders for a moment, his eyes dark with desire. Then his hands slipped beneath the surface of the water, moving slowly, exploringly down her skin until they came to her bikini top. His fingers moved over the wet material first, gently, caressingly, but with that touch of experience and sureness that had always driven her wild in the past. Carina gasped as she felt her body rise in awareness, and she made an involuntary movement to step away, but by then he had slipped her top down and his bare, wet hands were on her breasts. She shuddered, but became still again, closing her eyes as he went on caressing her, toying with her, leaving trails of minute air bubbles on her pouting breasts.

Carina sighed with pleasure, aroused not only by what he was doing to her, but by the fact that he was doing it here, surrounded by so many people. Opening her eyes, she looked up at Luis and saw his face taut with need. 'I want you, *cara*,' he said in a thick, harsh voice. 'I've never stopped wanting you,' he went on, his fingers becoming more urgent, until Carina began to pant and gasp, her breathing ragged as desire heightened.

Luis's hands slid down to her waist and he pulled her against him, pressing his hips against hers so that she could feel his hard, vibrant manhood, even here in the water. His closeness electrified her own desire, filling her with that familiar, aching emptiness. With a moan of frustration, Carina thrust her hips forward, moving voluptuously, Luis's hands tight on her hips. Beads of sweat broke out on her lips, despite the coolness of the water, and her hands gripped his waist, her nails digging unknowingly into his flesh.

'Say it,' Luis said urgently into her ear. 'Say that you still feel the same, too. Say that you . . .'

He pushed her away from him, so suddenly that Carina overbalanced and fell backwards into the sea. She came up, spluttering and hardly knowing where she was. Luis was still standing there, and trying to conceal a look of angry chagrin as Kurt and Stella came swimming up.

'Hi. Isn't the water gorgeous?' Stella said happily, but luckily didn't wait for Carina to answer before pointing to the rock island. 'Did you see us swim round it? I began to be afraid I wouldn't be able to do it, but Kurt helped me. He's a marvellous swimmer.'

She chattered on while Carina managed to wriggle herself back into her bikini top. For a few moments she'd felt completely disorientated, and almost as angry as Luis, but now she began to thank her lucky stars for the interruption. She must have been mad to let him touch her like that! Mad—or hypnotised all over again by the overwhelming sexual attraction she'd always felt for him.

Her face flushed with embarrassment as Carina realised just how wantonly she had behaved, and she turned to swim away from the others, putting all her strength into a fast crawl across the bay. If anything, the feeling of frustration was worse than ever now; her blood on fire, her teeth gritted together, she pushed herself through the water, deliberately tiring herself so that she would be too exhausted to feel anything.

The others had gone back to the shade when she came out. As Carina walked towards them, she found herself unable to look at Luis and had to keep her eyes fixed on Stella. The sun had started to slip behind the cliffs now, and a lot of people were packing up and leaving the beach. Picking up her towel, Carina stood with her back to Luis to shake off the sand and towel herself dry. 'Let's go back, shall we? It will probably take at least an hour to sail back to the villa.'

Everyone agreed and they collected their things. Carina managed to avoid looking into Luis's face, until she had no choice when he helped her aboard the boat from the dinghy. She had expected to see a triumphant look in his eyes at her easy capitulation to his touch, but was surprised to see him give her a smile that was full of tenderness. Her heart skipped a beat as Carina took her seat in the bow. She had been ready to be very angry, but now she felt strangely uncertain and vulnerable, almost as she had all those years ago when she had first met Luis and been so overpowered by him. Not only physically, but also by his certainty that they were in love and should marry. She had put her entire trust in Luis then, but of course it hadn't worked out. So had her trust been misplaced? It had always seemed so, but now Carina began to realise that perhaps her own pride had contributed to the break-up. If she hadn't been so determined to be a good wife and not bother him with her troubles when he was so busy, then he might have been able to save the marriage. Marriage, she realised, meant sharing, not shielding, as she had done. She had let everything build up until it had become unbearable, and had only then gone to him and begged him to find them a home of their own. No wonder Luis hadn't taken her seriously, when he had had no prior warning. But she had wanted to share only the good things, not the bad, and only now realised just how selfish that had been.

The sun started to set as they sailed gently back along the coast. Leaning back against the side of the boat, Carina watched the great blaze of orange and red that filled the western sky, a glorious finale of colour that made a fitting end to such a lovely day. As she watched it, she saw just how small her own world and problems were in the scheme of things. Looking at the crimson of the dying sun reflected off the high cliffs and the endless sea made her feel very unimportant, and yet very grateful that she was a part of it. She found a great comfort in the thought that, no matter what happened, the sun would rise again tomorrow and begin another day.

The boat turned, as Luis put the helm over and they began to enter the little bay below the villa. Carina glanced up and found Luis watching her. Their eyes met and, for the first time since she'd returned to Portugal, she gave him a wide, happy smile, full of warmth and friendliness.

They all laughed and chattered as they unloaded the boat and climbed up to the villa, then took it in turns to use the two bathrooms to bathe and change in before walking into the nearby fishing village for a meal. Afterwards, they went on to a disco where Kurt had a little too much to drink. As they walked back to the villa through the star-filled night, he started trying to teach them a song in Dutch, and they all became helpless with laughter at their attempts to copy his accent.

'You do not do it left,' Kurt complained, losing his English. 'Now you listen again.'

'Oh, no,' Stella groaned. 'Not again. Lord, it's so hot, I need a swim. Come on, Kurt, I'll race you back to the villa. Last one in the pool is a cissy.'

In the state Kurt was in, he probably didn't understand the exact words, but he certainly got the message. With a whoop, he took off after Stella, who was already a hundred yards up the road.

'I really don't think he ought to swim after all that drink,' Carina said worriedly. 'He might pass out and drown. Let's go after him.'

But Luis caught her arm. 'He'll be all right. Stella will look after him.' His steps slowed. 'I've hardly had a chance to be alone with you all day.'

Remembering what had happened when they *had* been comparatively alone, Carina flushed. 'I don't ...' she began, but stopped when Luis put his finger over her lips.

'Why don't we go down to the beach?' he suggested insinuatingly. She began to shake her head in refusal, but he said quickly, 'We'll talk. Just talk.'

Carina went to say that there was nothing to talk about, but realised that wasn't true any more. Taking hold of his wrist she pulled his finger away from her mouth, resisting a sudden urge to bite it. 'I don't want to go down to the beach,' she told him in sudden nervousness. 'I—I'm not sure that I even want to talk.'

'We'll walk, then.' Linking her arm in his, he held it firmly. 'Do you remember that cave in the hillside I once took you to?'

'Your boyhood bolt-hole, do you mean? Yes, I—I remember it.' Carina did, indeed. One day during their honeymoon, they had gone for a walk and been unable to get back to the villa before a violent storm had broken; but Luis had remembered the cave and taken her there to shelter. They hadn't been able to avoid the rain entirely, so Carina's dress and Luis's shirt were soaked through and clinging to them by the time they had reached it . . .

The entrance to the cave was tall and narrow, but inside it opened out to about eight feet high and twelve feet long, though it was only five or six feet wide. It was cool inside after the heat of the sun and Carina began to shiver as she looked around. 'How did you know this place was here? You can hardly see the entrance with those bushes around it.'

'I found it when I was a boy. I used to come here and wait until the heat had died down whenever I upset my parents.' His hands went to the straps of her dress. 'You'd better take this off or you'll get cold.'

She let him take off her wet dress, but said teasingly, 'And I always thought you were the most perfect child.'

'Well, you were wrong.' His hands began to explore her, his voice thickening at the still novel excitement of being able to touch and take her any time he wanted. 'Oh, Carina, *meu amor*, I love you so very much.' Taking off his wet shirt, he held her close against him, putting his arms round her to keep her warm. 'You're so beautiful, *cara*. So lovely.' He began to kiss her, but soon kisses weren't enough and they lay down together on the floor of the cave.

Her shivers of cold changed to tremors of desire, as Luis kissed and fondled her in growing passion. Outside,

the storm still raged, the lightning piercing the dark sky
and setting fire to the foaming waves of the sea. Rain
beat against the soft sandstone of the rocky hillside,
beating an endless tattoo that was lost beneath the
throbbing of Carina's heart and the growing tide of
ecstasy that filled her mind and body. The noise of the
storm was merely a background to their own passion, a
wildness of the elements that was as primitive as their
own hunger for each other's body. Only once was Carina
aware of it.

Vividly, she remembered that Luis had held back for a
moment and she had opened her eyes to see him poised
above her, his hair dishevelled, sweat on his brow, and
the tautness of desire in his face. She lay naked beneath
him, her hair an aureole of gold on the dusty floor of the
cave, her mouth parted, her breath an uneven moan of
longing. 'Luis!' She reached up for him, wanting his
closeness, wanting him to quench the fires that raged
through her veins.

Softly he stroked her cheek, his eyes dark and intense,
his breathing ragged. 'I love you,' he said on a sudden
fierce note of overwhelming emotion. 'I shall always love
you. So much. So much.'

'And I you, my darling. Oh, Luis!' Again she reached
up for him. 'I want always to be a part of you. I want you
to go on loving me for ever. Don't ever stop. Don't ever
. . .' Her voice broke off as Luis came down on her, his
hard body giving her the pleasure she craved. She cried
out, 'Oh, yes! Yes!' And arched her body towards him,
to greedily take his love as urgently as he gave it.

Afterwards, when they lay spent and exhausted in
each other's arms, life had seemed so wonderful that she
had been suddenly afraid and had clung to Luis in fear.

'Don't ever leave me! Promise you'll never leave me?'

'I won't, I swear it.' He held her tightly. 'You're mine and I'm yours. We'll always be together. Don't be afraid, *meu amor*, we'll always have each other . . .'

Now these words came echoing back to Carina through the years, just as they had echoed in the little cave. They had been as hollow as the cave too, she realised, although they had meant them then. But, stronger than the words, came back the memory of the emotions she had felt, and of the love they had shared. A love that had been so foolishly thrown away.

Luis paused as they walked along and looked into her eyes. Carina's face was lit by the soft light of the moon, its silver rays turning her hair to white-gold and revealing her thoughts to his gaze. 'Yes,' he said softly. 'You do remember.' His hand tightened on hers, and he looked down at her with the dark tautness of desire that she remembered so well. 'Let's go to the cave,' he said huskily. 'Will you come with me, Carina?'

Her fingers trembled in his, and for a moment she didn't speak. She knew what she must say, of course; to say anything but no would be wrong and utterly stupid. But when she opened her mouth to say it nothing came out. Her voice seemed to have become lost in time, in the deep pools of Luis's eyes, and in the still quietness of the night. After a long moment, Carina gave a deep sigh. 'Yes,' she breathed. 'I'll come with you.'

CHAPTER SIX

THE path to the cave seemed narrower than Carina remembered, and Luis had to help her down the steepest part. The bushes growing near the entrance seemed thicker, too, as Luis pushed them aside, letting the moonlight shine into the cave.

'Have you—have you been back here since?'

'No. I told you, I haven't been coming to the villa.' Luis stood by the entrance, where there was a sort of ledge that looked out over the bay. From here they could see the villa in the far distance, lights shining from some of the windows and from the floodlights round the pool.

They were both silent for a few moments, neither in any hurry to go into the cave. But presently Luis looked inside it again and said, 'Have we changed so much since then, Carina? It's only four years, that isn't so long, surely?'

'Sometimes it seems like a lifetime. I know I've become harder, but I'm not ashamed of that. And I think that ...' She hesitated, finding it difficult to describe. 'Perhaps I've become colder,' she said slowly. 'Just like you said. I don't find it easy to—form relationships any more.'

'With men?' Luis asked swiftly.

'Yes, with men. I've certainly never felt like marrying anyone else.

'I'm flattered,' Luis said and moved nearer to her, but Carina stepped away, suddenly angry.

'Well, you shouldn't be. You should be damn well ashamed! I was an extrovert until I met you, but now I always try to hide my feelings, because I'm afraid of getting hurt again. It's only this last year or so that I've even begun to feel more at ease when I'm with a man.' She gave a tight laugh. 'Possibly because I've become so good at saying no.'

'Always? Do you always say no?' This time, Luis wasn't to be denied. He took hold of her arm and turned her to face him.

She looked up at him for a moment, his features chiselled by the moonlight, giving him a lean and hungry look. 'It matters to you a great deal, doesn't it—whether or not I've been with other men?'

Lifting his free hand, he took hold of her other arm as well, as if by holding her he could better emphasise what he was about to say. 'We've been apart for over four years,' he said fiercely. 'Do you know how many days that is? How many nights? It's over fifteen hundred. For more than fifteen hundred nights I've lain alone in my bed—and there hasn't been one night that has gone by without me thinking about you, without me wishing you were there beside me. For sex, yes. But because I love and need you, too. Do you know how many times I've woken up and reached out for you, only to go, all over again, through the hell of realising that you're not there?' His voice roughened. 'And then comes the even worse hell when I start wondering where you are, whether you're with someone else. I remember all the wonderful things we did together, and I start picturing you with someone else.'

'Stop it!' Carina's voice cut through his. 'Do you think that I wasn't going through the same sort of mental torture? I used to think of all those well-born Portuguese girls your mother was always telling me she'd hoped you would have married, and imagine you—you . . .'

'What?' Luis's hands tightened. 'Imagine me what?'

'M-making love to them.' She wrestled herself free and turned her back on him. 'But I'm not going to ask you whether you've been with one of them or—or anyone. Because I don't want to know. I'm—I'm not interested.'

'Oh, but I think you are.' Coming up behind her, Luis slid his hands round her waist. Bending his dark head, he began to lightly kiss her shoulder. 'You may have changed in some ways, perhaps we both have, but there's one thing that has stayed the same. And that's this instantaneous physical attraction for each other that we both feel. No matter how you try, *minha cara*, you can't deny that.'

His lips moved along to her neck, and Carina wanted to cry out at the sheer hedonistic pleasure of it. 'No,' she admitted. 'I can't. Though I did try, I really did. But when you took me into the water this afternoon, I—I wanted you to make love to me there and then.'

'I know.' His lips found the lobe of her ear and began to nibble at it, and his hands moved up from her waist to cup her breasts.

Carina's breath caught in her throat. 'Were you—did you really spend all those nights alone?'

Lifting his mouth from her neck, Luis said softly, 'I swear it. I've always thought of myself as still married to you, and I've kept the vows I made you. You're the only woman in my life, Carina. The only one I will ever want.'

He turned her to face him as he spoke, then took her in his arms and kissed her deeply. 'And you?' he asked afterwards, his voice tightening. 'Please tell me the truth, Carina.'

She gave a small smile and lifted her hand to gently stroke his cheek. 'I ought to punish you by telling you there were dozens—and all of them far better lovers than you'll ever be. But it wouldn't be true. No man could be a better lover than you—for me, anyway. I suppose that's really why it was so difficult for me to ever be at ease with men; I was always comparing them to you and finding that they just didn't measure up.' She smiled into his slowly widening eyes. 'No, Luis, you're the only man who's ever made love to me. I admit that a couple of times I came pretty close, but something always held me back, made me realise that it wasn't right.'

'Oh, my love, you'll never know how happy that makes me! I'd almost given up hope of your ever coming back to me.' Pulling her gently closer, Luis put his arms round her and kissed her, enveloping her in his warmth and love.

Carina returned his kiss ardently, losing herself in his embrace, feeling the hot glow of happiness spreading through her. It felt so right to be back in his arms; it was where she belonged, where she should always have stayed. She murmured his name against his mouth on a sigh of mingled relief and thankfulness; tears came into her eyes and she moved her head against his shoulder, clinging to him tightly, overcome by emotion.

'Oh, *cara, meu amor*.' He spoke soothing words of comfort to her in his own language, holding her close and gently stroking her hair. 'It's all right, my little love. We're together. Nothing can part us now. Never again.'

He kissed her again, insistently. Kissed the teardrops from her cheeks and eyelashes, kissed her trembling lips until he had aroused passion in her once more. His breathing unsteady, Luis drew her towards the mouth of the cave and lifted the bushes aside for her to enter. 'Come,' he said thickly. 'I want you, Carina. I want you now, my heart's desire.'

'Oh, Luis.' Carina stood close beside him and looked into the cave. The moonlight lay across the floor, lighting the soft dust of sand which covered it, and it seemed almost as if she could still see the marks left where they had lain that last time, during the storm. They had been so happy then, had been so sure of their bright future. Now she had only to step past the bushes and it would become a bower of love all over again. She would be held in Luis's arms, feel his touch, so familiar and yet so new, have this aching void in her body filled at last.

'Come,' Luis said again, his voice urgent now. 'I've waited so long for you to come back to me. I yearn to hold you in my arms again.'

But still Carina hesitated from taking that decisive step into the cave. 'I want you, too,' she told him sincerely. 'So *very* much. But I . . .' She glanced again at the cave and shook her head. 'But I can't. Not yet. It wouldn't be right.'

'Why not? We're married.' Luis stepped into the cave, and tried to draw her after him.

'No, I can't.' Carina hung back. 'Luis, please try to understand. If I—go in there with you, if we make love, then I'll have committed myself to you all over again.'

'But that's what I want,' he said urgently. 'I told you I

wanted you to come back to me. I *want* us to live together again.'

'But can't you see? Nothing's changed. Your mother is still living at your house. It would all begin again, just as it did before. Unless—unless you'd promise to find somewhere else for us, a house of our own.' She looked up at him pleadingly, but her heart sank when she saw his features harden.

'My mother is ill, Carina. I can't just walk out on her.'

'Not even for me, so that we can live together happily? Spend the rest of our lives together?'

Luis's face twisted. 'Are you making conditions, Carina? Must I give up my mother for you?'

'I'm not asking that. I'm only asking that you give us a chance. I'm sorry, Luis, but I could never feel happy or—or relaxed if I had to live in the same house as your mother again.'

'All right.' He had moved out of the cave and leaned against the rock at the entrance, his hands in his pockets. 'I'll find an apartment for us in Lisbon. I can't move my mother out of the house, that would be cruel, and you'll have to accept that I'll have to see her regularly. But I want us to be together. And I want you to be happy. I want those things more than anything in the world.'

'So do I.' Moving forward, Carina put her hands on his waist. 'But you must promise me something else, Luis. I've said that I don't want you to give up your mother, but I don't want you to let her poison your mind against me. And she'll try, I know she will. She—she's always hated me.'

Taking his hands from his pockets, Luis put them on her shoulders. 'Don't worry, I won't let anything come between us.' His hands tightened. 'I'd do anything to keep you, now that I've found you again. If I lost you after this, life would be unbearable.'

'Thank you.' Leaning forward, Carina lifted her head to kiss him. 'You won't be sorry. I promise.'

He smiled. 'And nor will you, *cara*. That, too, is a promise—and one I would like to keep as soon as possible.'

Carina chuckled and moved close to him, her arms round his waist. 'I can't wait for us to be together. I'll have to go back to England, of course, to . . .' She felt a sudden tension in his body and broke off. 'Oh, only to re-let my flat and collect my things. There's a girl who works at my agency who I can put in charge of it, but I don't intend to let it go completely.' She saw the look on his face and smiled. 'Well, not quite yet, anyway.'

'Why don't you start a translation agency here?' Luis suggested.

'It's an idea, although so many Portuguese people already speak English. The other way round is unusual. But I don't want to be left alone all day with nothing to do.'

'Well, maybe I can do something about that, too, before very long,' Luis said meaningfully as he bent to kiss her neck.

'Does that mean what I think it does?' Carina asked on an unsteady note.

'Of course, what else?' Putting his hands on either side of her face, Luis said earnestly, 'I want us to be man and wife again. I want to give you children, to make up for the years we've lost. Those years have been the loneliest in my life. It's as if I was torn apart, my body functioning here, but my heart in England with you. I

want to be whole again, and I can only be that with you.'
He paused, his eyes holding hers. 'But you, too, must
make me a promise, Carina. If you come back to me,
then you must stay. I couldn't go through that hell
again. I'll do whatever you want, but you must swear
never to leave me—and that there isn't anyone else.'

'There isn't, I've told you.' She kissed him again.
'And I swear I won't leave you. If you like, I'll even
follow you to Lisbon tomorrow to start looking for an
apartment. Then we can be together all the sooner. I'll
have to go back to my hotel first to collect my things, but
I'll only be a few hours behind you.'

'I *do* like that. I'd like it very much.' Luis returned her
kiss, but when she opened her eyes Carina realised that
she could hardly see his face, it had grown so dark. Luis,
too, looked up at the sky. 'The moon's going in. We'd
better get back up the hillside while we're still able to
see.'

He looked regretfully at the cave for a moment, but
Carina took his hand and said, 'Don't worry. There'll be
plenty more opportunities.' She gave a happy laugh.
'After all, we still have our second honeymoon to
arrange.'

'Yes—and somehow I think it's going to be even more
exciting than our first,' Luis agreed, his laughter
echoing hers.

The climb back up the hill was more difficult in the
dark, but Carina felt no fear when Luis was with her to
guide her footsteps and help her over the steep parts. It
became instead an adventure and they laughed a lot,
becoming young and crazy again. When they reached
the more level path and then the road, they didn't hurry
back to the villa, instead making plans as they walked

slowly along, stopping often to kiss or just hold each other.

'It seems silly to travel back to Lisbon separately,' Luis said eagerly. 'Why don't we go back together in my car and leave yours here for Stella and Kurt to use for a while, and then take back to the hire company?'

'That sounds fine, but I still have to check out of the hotel. Are you sure it won't make you late getting back to Lisbon?'

'Not if we set out early. My first client isn't due until eleven, but if I'm late he'll just have to wait.'

'Wow!' Carina opened her eyes wide in mock amazement. 'That doesn't sound like your usual conscientious self. Anybody would think you were in love, or something.'

'And they would be right.' Luis agreed, his voice thickening as he stopped and pulled her to him. 'Oh, Carina, I can't wait to show you just how much I love you. How much I need you.'

'I can't wait either, but—please, not tonight, not at the villa with Stella and Kurt there.'

'No, I wouldn't want that either. We'll wait till tomorrow and find a hotel somewhere. Though how I'm going to concentrate on work until then ...'

Carina laughed softly and moved against him, arousing him to instant awareness. 'Maybe this will help?'

'No, it damn well won't! It just makes me want to throw you on the ground and take you here and now.'

'But you're too civilised, huh?' she teased, pressing harder.

Luis groaned and pushed her away. 'Don't tempt me.'

But then he drew her back again. 'But on second thoughts ...'

She laughed richly. 'Trouble is, I may be getting the worst of this—or the best, of course.'

They had reached the dim light of a street lamp, and Luis smiled down at her as he held her. 'Oh, Carina, my sweet, how could we have been such fools? In future, if anything—however small—goes wrong, we must promise to talk it through. *Sim?*'

'*Sim,*' Carina agreed. 'But in English or Portuguese?'

'Both,' Luis smiled. 'It's wonderful that you kept up your lessons. Now you won't feel so strange here. Why did you?' he asked curiously. 'I thought, when you went away, that you wanted nothing more to do with Portugal.'

Carina shook her head. 'I don't know, really. Maybe it was because in my heart I always hoped this would happen. And maybe that was why I let my mother persuade me to come here so easily. Even though I didn't realise it myself.' She looked at Luis, suddenly anxious. 'It will work this time, won't it? Promise me it will.'

'I promise,' Luis soothed, picking up her hand and kissing it. 'Nothing can separate us now.'

So they walked slowly on, discussing how soon Luis could take some time off from his practice so that they could have another honeymoon, and where would be the best part of Lisbon to try to find a place to live. Around them, the noise of crickets filled the air, mingling with the sound of the waves breaking on the beach below the cliffs. But they were too engrossed in each other to hear, or to notice that the night was beginning to lighten until they reached the villa and found it still and dark. Only then did Luis look at his watch and say, 'Good heavens, it's almost four-thirty.'

'Hardly worth going to bed, then.'

'No, we must try and get some sleep. It's a long drive to Lisbon.'

'But we can share it,' Carina reminded him.

Luis looked at her and smiled, taking her hand. 'Yes, for a moment I'd forgotten that I'll be sharing my life again.'

'And your bed,' she reminded him coquettishly.

'If you shared my bed now, neither of us would get any sleep.'

She smiled. 'No, I suppose not. Goodnight, then, Luis.'

Carina held out her hand to him, but he pulled her into his arms and kissed her with uncontrolled hunger, leaving her feeling almost giddy. 'Dream about me,' Luis said thickly. 'And now, for God's sake, go to bed before I forget myself completely.'

With a low laugh she obeyed him, but was so happy and excited that she thought going to bed a complete waste of time—but then remembered nothing else until Luis tapped lightly on her door at six-thirty.

Carina stirred and muttered something, but was still more than half asleep as he came into the room. He stood for a moment looking down at her in the half-light from the shuttered windows, at her dishevelled hair and the long lashes of her closed eyes brushing her cheeks. She moved again, slowly and reluctantly surfacing towards wakefulness, and the thin cotton sheet that covered her slipped further down, revealing her bare shoulders and one rounded breast. Luis caught his breath, and the next moment was on his knees beside the bed. Gently, he reached and took hold of the sheet, drawing it slowly down the length of the bed until Carina's slim, firm young body lay exposed before him.

For a few minutes he didn't touch her, merely feasted his eyes once more on the soft curves he had loved to caress, on the silky skin that he had kissed so many times that he knew her body as intimately as she did herself. She was as beautiful as he remembered, lovelier, perhaps, her slim girlishness having ripened into womanhood so that her breasts were a little fuller, her stomach above the soft golden hairs a little more rounded. He loved her body so much. Only the thought of another man having known it had kept him away from her all these years. Luis remembered the first time he had taken her, when she had been a virgin and afraid, but so brave and passionate that it had been a time of the greatest ecstasy for them both. He had wanted her so badly then, almost as badly as he wanted her now. The familiar, yearning ache filled his loins, and his hands were trembling as he at last reached out to touch her.

He began at her feet, gently stroking, his hands as tender as if he were touching a child. Carina felt them on her, and came a little more awake, straightening her body and turning her head towards him. She gave a low purr of sensuous pleasure, her eyes still closed, feeling as if she was having the most wonderful dream. Luis's hands travelled upwards, exploring her kneecaps, finding them enchanting, and then moving on. As his fingers travelled up her legs and began to fondle her, Carina's purr of pleasure changed to a gasp and her eyes flew open, fully awake at last.

Luis felt the tension in her body, but his eyes stayed on what he was doing. 'Lie still,' he said softly. He bent to kiss her, deeply, lingeringly, until she was quivering with desire. But then his hands moved on to stroke her stomach, span her waist, taking his time and recalling every inch of her body to his memory and present delight. When he reached her breasts and found them fully aroused, he kissed her again, sucking and gently biting her nipples until she shuddered and began to moan softly, her fingers digging into the mattress in the effort not to cry out with excitement.

When at last Luis raised his head, Carina's brow was wet with perspiration, her body trembling and her eyes wide with yearning. 'Oh Luis, I wish . . .'

'Tonight,' he said softly, kissing her. 'Tonight we'll make love the whole night through.'

'Oh, *yes*! Yes.' She clung to him for a few minutes, until her heart had steadied a little, then lifted her head to look at him with a smile. 'Tomorrow morning,' she threatened, 'I'm going to do that to you.'

Luis laughed delightedly. 'In that case, I shall never get to the office.' Unable to resist, he reached out to caress her again, his eyes on her face this time, watching the sensuousness that grew in her eyes and opened her lips in a pout of pure sexuality. 'Soon,' he said hoarsely. 'Soon we'll have that second honeymoon and we'll be together all day and all night. I'll be able to hold you, kiss you, love you . . . Oh, Carina, *cara*, I love you so much.' His arms tightened around her, and for a brief moment he held her so tightly that she could hardly breathe. Then he stood up abruptly. 'I must let you get dressed. Coffee in ten minutes and we'll get breakfast somewhere on the road.'

'All right.' Carina sat up on the edge of the bed and watched him go to the door, but when he reached it, as she'd guessed he would, he was unable to resist looking back at her.

She smiled at him, her eyes loving, and Luis grinned back, his face full of happiness again and looking years younger than he had that first day. It was wonderful, that smile; it made Carina feel warm and happy and safe, sure of her future again instead of being in limbo as she had been in the last few years.

It didn't take long to dress—Carina still had only her shorts and suntop to wear. She would have to change when she got to the hotel. As she brushed her hair, Carina looked at her reflection in the mirror and her hand slowed. She looked so happy, her eyes sparkling, that she had to smile at herself and then laugh aloud. Today was going to be the most wonderful day of her life, she just knew it was. She might even be lucky enough to find a furnished apartment they could move into today, so that they could have the place to themselves. Even if she couldn't, there would always be a hotel room somewhere. And it didn't matter where, any place would do so long as tonight they could renew, with bodily love, those vows they had made so long ago—and in their hearts had never really broken.

Luis was standing in the kitchen, drinking his coffee when she joined him. He gave her a mug and slipped his arm round her waist, not saying anything, but smiling down into her eyes as they drank.

And that was how Stella found them when she came wandering sleepily into the kitchen a few mintues later. 'Is there any coffee to spare?' She blinked at them owlishly and then grinned. 'You two seem to have got quite friendly again since last night.'

Carina smiled back. 'You could say that—thanks to you.'

Stella looked very pleased with herself. 'It *was* clever of me, wasn't it? I just knew you two were pining away for each other,' she said on a soulful sigh.

Both Carina and Luis burst out laughing. 'We weren't as bad as that, surely?' Putting down her mug, Carina gave her sister a hug. 'Thanks,' she said sincerely. 'I'll always be grateful.'

'And I,' Luis said, kissing Stella too. 'It's time to go. I'll wait for you in the car, *cara*.'

'OK, I won't be a moment.' When he'd gone, Carina said, 'Look, I'm going back to Lisbon with Luis now.' She grimaced. 'I suppose I'll have to phone Mother and tell her what's happened as soon as I get there.'

'She isn't going to be pleased.'

'I know, but I'm afraid she'll just have to learn to live with it. But she's bound to ask me about you and Kurt—so what do I tell her?'

Stella laughed. 'Just tell her that it's only a holiday friendship, after all, and that I'll be home in time to start university.'

'Well, that's a blessing—I'll be able to give her the bad news first, but then counter it with the good news.'

'And just what do you think she'll take as the good, yours or mine?'

'Yours of course. She hated the idea of my living abroad, and she never liked Luis.'

'You shouldn't worry about Mum. You've got your own life to lead.'

'I most certainly don't intend to, not any more. And this time it's going to be for keeps, I just know it.' Carina gave Stella an impulsive hug. 'Oh, Stell, I'm so happy!'

'So you should be—after a night making it up with Luis.'

Carina blushed laughingly. 'Oh, we haven't made it up quite that much yet. We spent too long talking and ironing things out. But tonight,' she blushed again, 'tonight, we'll really make it up.'

A car horn sounded outside, and she quickly ran to join Luis and drive the few miles to her hotel.

'Did you ask her about Kurt?' Luis asked as they drove along roads not yet busy with traffic, the air still clear and with the faint tang of the ocean.

'Yes, it was as I expected; she's not at all serious about him. He's just a friend she was using as an excuse to get me back here.'

'Thank God she did.' Luis's hand reached out to cover hers as it lay on her lap, and he smiled at her. Then he glanced at his watch. 'We're running late. I hope they don't keep us waiting too long at your hotel.'

When they reached it, the square in front of the hotel was only just beginning to come to life, with a few holidaymakers sitting having breakfast at the café on the beach and the local people opening their shops. Searching around in her bag, Carina said, 'I don't think I handed in my key. No, here it is.'

'I'll come up with you while you pack and carry your case down.'

'OK.' Carina leant across and kissed him. 'It's going to be nice having a man around again.'

Luis returned her kiss avidly. 'Just nice?'

'I don't want to make you big-headed.'

He wrinkled his nose at her. 'Go on—make me big-headed.'

'All right.' She slid her arms round his neck. 'Having

you around again is going to be wonderful, marvellous, fantastic, dreamy, sensational ...' She ran out of adjectives. 'There! Satisfied?'

'No.' He smiled into her eyes, his own warm and tender. 'I'll never be satisfied—of having you.' And after that, of course, there was no way he could resist kissing her yet again. But after a few moments Luis lifted his head and groaned. 'I'm sorry, but I just have to get back to Lisbon.'

'I know.'

They hurried into the hotel, but there was no one at the desk. Carina banged on the bell a couple of times and after a moment Luis said, 'Give me your key, I'll go and start packing for you.'

'All right. The room is on the second floor. Turn right at the top of the stairs.' She pressed the bell again and this time the receptionist came hurrying to the desk. '*Sim, senhora?*'

'Could you make out my bill please? I'm leaving immediately.'

'Of course, *senhora*.' He caught sight of Luis taking the stairs two at a time. 'But who is ...'

'Oh, that's my husband,' Carina told him, and turned to hurry after Luis.

'But—but *senhora* ...' The man stared at her, an arm raised as if to call her back.

'It's all right—he hasn't been staying here,' Carina told him, thinking that the man might have thought they were cheating the hotel. Although why they should, Carina didn't know. After all, she'd had to agree to pay the full price for the double room.

Luis was some way ahead of her when she reached the top of the stairs. She saw him unlock her door to go into the room, and by the time she reached the door he was at the window, pulling back the curtain. He turned to speak to her and then stopped abruptly, staring at the bed nearest the window. Carina followed his gaze and her mouth dropped open. There was a man in her room! For a ghastly moment she thought Luis had got the wrong room, and she looked guiltily at the door, but no, it was the right number. Then she thought that the hotel must have given her up when she hadn't been back for two nights, and let her room to someone else. She was about to back out of the room to have a hell of a row with the management when the man in the bed wakened and turned over. He sat up and Carina nearly died—it was Greg Summers!

'Carina? Hey, where have you been? I've been waiting for . . .' His voice died away as he saw Luis. 'Oh! I—er—wasn't expecting you.'

'Obviously not!' Luis's voice was glacial. He tossed the key on the spare bed and strode towards the door, his eyes flaming in contemptuous fury.

'Luis! Luis, I didn't know he was going to be here.' From somewhere, Carina found her voice and stammered out a protest. But Luis merely glared at her murderously and pushed her aside as he marched out.

'Luis!' Carina ran after him and caught his arm. 'For God's sake, *I didn't know he was there*! Do you think I would have left him here? Do you think I would have let you come here?' She was talking much too fast, almost incoherently in her urgency, but Luis was taking no notice of her, his face thunderous as he began to hurry down the stairs. Running in front of him, Carina put up her arms to bar his way. 'Will you please listen to me?'

'What the hell difference would it make?' Luis spat

out savagely. 'Whether you knew he was there or not, it's obvious that you lied to me. If he knows you well enough to wait for you in your room, you must have had an affair with him. You must have been lovers!'

'That isn't true! Luis, please, come back with me. Ask him what he's doing there. I'm sure he ...'

Luis's voice cut through her pleas in a harsh laugh. 'It's perfectly obvious what he was doing there—he was waiting for you to join him in bed. But I spoilt it by insisting on coming back with you, didn't I?'

He pushed past her again, but Carina grabbed his arm. A man came along, staring at them as he went down to breakfast. 'It isn't like that. I told you, I ...'

But Luis swung round on her. 'We could have slept together last night, and you could have come straight from my bed to his!'

'No! I would never ... How could you even *think* that?'

'I'm beginning to think a hell of a lot of things about you. I ought to have known that anyone who looks like you couldn't have stayed faithful all these years.' Roughly, he pushed her aside and went on down the stairs.

The receptionist was in the lobby, agog with curiosity, but Carina ignored him as she followed Luis out to the car. Even as she followed him she knew that hope was gone. He was so furiously angry, so hurt and humiliated, that none of her arguments or pleas could get through to him. But she had to make one last try. Catching hold of the car door when he opened it, she pushed herself in the way and caught hold of his jacket. 'Luis, listen. I *love* you. I want to live with you again. And I told you the *truth*. I'm not having an affair with

Greg. I only met him last week and I ...'

But Luis gave her a scathing look that made her shrink inside and thrust her out of the way as if she was something disgustingly dirty. 'Sorry,' he said viciously, 'the offer is no longer open. But I shall be taking you up on *your* offer—of a divorce! Because I never want to see you again!' And he gunned the engine, accelerating fast out of the square and disappearing up the road in a cloud of dust.

Carina stood there for several minutes, watching him go, then turned and walked down to the beach and across the sand to the sea, tears of despair running down her face.

CHAPTER SEVEN

'ARE you ever going to speak to me again?'

Greg's voice broke through her unhappiness, and Carina turned to see him squatting on the beach a couple of yards behind her, his legs drawn up and his arms resting on his knees. 'How long have you been here?'

'Quite some time. You seemed—preoccupied.'

She gave a grim smile and bent to pick up a handful of little pebbles, sending them skimming almost viciously across the surface of the sea.

'You're good at that,' Greg said admiringly. She didn't answer, so after a few minutes he said, 'Look, I'm sorry. Will you let me explain?'

'Does it matter? Does anything matter?' Carina said bitterly.

'If I tell you what happened, then you can tell Luis.'

'It's too late, he won't listen. Not now.'

She still had her back to him and Greg couldn't see her face properly, but every line of her body showed deep dejection. 'There was nothing going on in Lisbon,' he began on an explanatory note. 'Nothing to do with my business partnership, that is. I missed you,' he added bluntly. 'I wanted to see you again. I must have phoned your hotel a dozen times, but they always said you weren't there, that they hadn't seen you for some time. The language was a problem; I wasn't sure whether or not you'd checked out. So I decided to come down here and look for you. When I got here, I wanted to check

140

your room, make sure you were OK, but they wouldn't let me. So I told them I was your husband.'

Carina turned to stare at him. 'You did *what*?'

Greg held up his hands. 'I know. I know. I had no right to do it. But I'd got this idea in my head that you were lying there ill or something, especially when they said they hadn't seen you for so long. It's only a small hotel—I didn't trust them.' He looked at her. 'I wasn't going to take any chances. Not where you're concerned. Well, anyway,' he looked across at the horizon, 'you weren't there and your bed hadn't been slept in. So I waited for you. I hung around the hotel and this village all yesterday afternoon and evening, but you still didn't show up. I didn't relish the drive back to Lisbon along that terrible road in the dark, so I decided to stay here the night—but there wasn't an empty room available— and they all seemed to expect me, as your husband, to share your room—so I did,' he finished simply.

There was silence as Carina took it in; such a simple explanation to have ruined her life all over again. No wonder the receptionist had been so amazed when she'd said that Luis was her husband! The situation would have been very funny if it hadn't had such tragic results. 'I suppose I ought to be grateful to you for worrying about me.'

'But somehow I don't think you're ever going to forgive me for it.'

'No,' Carina agreed sadly, 'I don't think I ever will.'

There was a short, rather unpleasant silence, until Greg said, 'I take it you and your husband had got back together?'

'We were about to. We hadn't got much further than deciding that we wanted to, but we . . .' Her voice broke.

'We were going to try.'

'Oh, hell!' Greg got to his feet and shoved his hands into his pockets. 'Carina, I'm sorry. I didn't know. I wouldn't have had this happen for the world. Even though I like you so much, I wouldn't have wanted to get in the way of your happiness.' He saw her shoulders begin to shake, and he quickly went over and put his arms round her, letting her sob her heart out on his broad shoulder.

At length, she was quiet and put a hand up to wipe her eyes. 'Thanks. I'm sorry to be so—female. I must look terrible.'

Greg grinned and held her at arm's length, looking her over. 'Yes,' he agreed. 'You do.' Which made her smile a little. 'That's better. Have you had breakfast?'

Carina shook her head and he determinedly led her over to a little café with tables outside, sat her down, ordered a large English breakfast for her and made her eat it. He didn't let her talk until she'd finished the lot and was sitting back drinking a second cup of coffee, then he nodded approvingly. 'You're looking better. So—what do you intend to do now, Carina?'

She shook her head and put a hand up to her forehead. 'I haven't even begun to think. Go back to England, I suppose,' she answered dully.

'Is there no chance of making it up with your husband?'

Carina shook her head, remembering the fury in Luis's eyes.

'Are you sure? Supposing I go to see him, and tell him the truth?'

'He wouldn't listen. He's very—proud.'

'And pig-headed, by the sound of it,' Greg said

brusquely. He looked at her for a moment, then reached out to pick up her hand. 'Carina, are you sure this hasn't happened for the best? If he's the type of man who can just storm out of your life like that, without a word of explanation . . .'

'You don't understand,' Carina broke in. 'Please, I—I don't want to discuss it, discuss Luis.'

'All right. ' Greg let her take her hand away and sat back. 'So, let's get back to what you're going to do. Do you have to get back to England?'

She shrugged. 'What else is there?'

'How about taking on a job, here, in Portugal?'

Her eyes came up to look into his, suddenly wary. 'What kind of job?'

'As my interpreter,' Greg said easily. 'I'm having a hell of a time with this language, and it's going to be worse when we come to actually building the golf course. I could really use someone to help me.'

She shook her head. 'I'm sorry, it's out of the question. But thanks, anyway.'

'Why is it?' Greg persisted. He leaned forward. 'Just think about it for a moment. Do you really want to go back to England right now? Maybe it would do you good to have a breathing space. And if it's me you're worrying about—well, there aren't any strings to the offer, if that's what you're afraid of.'

Carina looked at his ruggedly handsome face; he certainly sounded sincere enough. 'You mean that this would be a purely business arrangement?'

He gave her one of his lazy grins. 'Well, it would certainly start off that way, but I have to admit that I definitely hope it would develop into something more.'

His grin was infectious and made her want to smile

back. 'I'd decided that I still loved my husband and wanted to go back to him,' she reminded Greg.

He nodded. 'I know. But after the way he's treated you . . .' He gave a slight shrug. 'Well, maybe you'll change your mind.'

She looked at him reflectively. She certainly liked Greg, liked him a lot, and if Luis hadn't come back into her life—well, who knew? Carina remembered the way she'd cried on Greg's shoulder. It had been the wrong shoulder, of course, but even so it had been a great comfort to have him there. On the other hand she felt no magnetism, no electricity, no instant attraction that set her body on fire as she did with Luis. But maybe that was for the best; she had been trying to avoid love, but the moment she had weakened and succumbed to it, it had slapped her in the face all over again.

And then there were all the practical problems; at the moment, she was stuck here without any transport. Carina supposed that she could phone up the villa and ask Stella to bring the hire car over, but that would mean having to tell her sister what had happened, and right now her emotions were so raw and bleeding that she shrank from having to make lengthy explanations. Which left the alternative of trying to hire another car in this fishing village or else getting a lift from Greg. 'Are you going back to Lisbon?' she asked him. He nodded. 'Can you give me a lift?'

'Of course. And the job?' His grey eyes were on her face, trying to guess what she was thinking.

Carina hesitated. 'I don't know. I'll have to think about it.'

'Fair enough. At least you haven't rejected the idea out of hand.' He stood up. 'Let's go over to the hotel and collect your cases. I think the sooner we get out of here, the better.'

Carina couldn't have agreed with him more. She hurriedly went up to her room and tried not to look at the bed where Greg had slept, while she packed her case as quickly as she could, just throwing the clothes in haphazardly. When she went down to the lobby, she found that Greg had already paid the bill and she was very grateful not to have to face the receptionist and the other staff who had come out to watch them go and were staring at them with open curiosity, a couple of the men even giving Carina leering smiles.

Her cheeks flushed in her otherwise pale face, Carina got into Greg's car and was never more glad to get away from a place in her life. She didn't speak until they were well clear of the village, then she said, 'How much do I owe you for my hotel bill?'

'Nothing, of course.' She opened her mouth to protest, but Greg said quickly, 'Look, Carina, don't argue. I used the room myself, remember?'

'As if I could forget!'

'Yeah. Well, why don't we try and forget about that?'

Which was asking the impossible, Carina thought gloomily as she sat back in her seat. She looked out of the window, but the passing scenery held no attraction for her now. Her thoughts were all on Luis and what might have been, and she was so dejected that she came to think of what had happened as some kind of punishment. She had thrown away her first chance of happiness with Luis, so now her second chance had been cruelly taken away from her.

They stopped for a coffee on the way back, but Carina sat listlessly looking down at her cup. Greg watched her

for a few minutes and then said shortly, 'Snap out of it,
Carina. You haven't lived with the man for years.
You've made another life for yourself and you can do it
again. You don't need him.'

'Don't I?'

'No. I'm sure of it.'

'And do I need you?'

'No, not really,' he admitted with blunt honesty. 'But
I think it will help to have a shoulder to cry on for a
while. And it will certainly help to have something to
occupy your mind and keep you busy.'

'I could be equally busy in England,' Carina pointed
out.

'Perhaps you could—during the days. But what about
the nights?'

'Are you saying that you want to occupy my nights?'
she asked stiffly.

'Only in so far as taking you out to dinner or to a dance
or whatever. The night stops at your bedroom door—
unless you ever care to invite me in,' he added
deliberately.

For a long moment, Carina studied his face, then
shook her head. 'I don't know.'

They continued their journey, finally arriving in
Lisbon around one o'clock. Greg drove straight to his
hotel and took out her case and his own overnight bag.
She walked with him into the hotel and up to the
reception desk, where he turned to her and said, 'OK, so
do I book you a room or an air ticket home?'

It was his mention of the word 'home' that finally
decided her. It conjured up an image of her mother, who
would be happy that Stella hadn't committed herself to
'some foreigner', and who would be more than

triumphant if she ever found out that she and Luis had broken up yet again. And right now Carina just couldn't take that. 'I'll stay,' Carina said decisively. 'I'll take the job.'

Greg grinned at her and touched her arm, but merely turned to the receptionist and said, 'I'd like to book an extra room for my secretary, please.'

From then on, and to Carina's relief, he became very businesslike. After they'd settled in their rooms, showered and changed and had lunch at the hotel restaurant, he gave her a whole pile of documents to go through to make sure that the English translation of them that he'd been given was correct. While she worked, he went over the plans for the clubhouse that was to be built on the site, and then dictated some letters for her to translate. 'We'd better try and hire a typewriter,' he decided.

'OK, I'll phone round and get one delivered.'

'You're very efficient,' Greg observed with a grin.

'That's what you're paying me for.' A thought occurred to her. 'You *are* going to pay me, aren't you?'

Greg roared with laughter. 'I wondered when you would get round to that.'

Carina smiled back, her mouth creasing at the corners; not much of a smile, but at least it *was* a smile.

'That's better.' Standing up, he took her hand. 'Come on, that's enough work for today. I need some exercise. Why don't we take a walk, and you can show me Lisbon?'

They walked for a long time, Greg's legs, used to striding miles across gold courses, never seeming to tire.

But Carina's eventually flagged, so they found a Chinese restaurant where they ate a leisurely meal, afterwards going back to the hotel. Greg was as good as his word, and left her at the door of her room, not that Carina had really been afraid that he would do anything else. Greg was a sensitive man; he wasn't going to push when he knew that all he would get was an instant rejection.

She eventually slept that night, and in the morning had an electric typewriter brought round and did the letters, plus some more for Greg's own business in England, where, it seemed, he had a financial interest in several companies. In the afternoon they went to a meeting with the architect who had designed the clubhouse, and later had dinner with the man that evening, Carina acting as interpreter for the two of them.

'I've another business meeting at ten tomorrow,' Greg told her as they parted that night. 'So I'll see you down at breakfast at nine.'

But it wasn't until they were in a taxi on their way to the meeting the next morning that Greg told her that it was another meeting of all the partners and their legal advisers.

'But that means . . .' Carina stared at him. 'It means Luis will be there!'

'Most probably,' Greg agreed.

Turning blindly, she made a grab at the doorhandle. 'Stop the taxi, I've got to get out. I can't possibly go!' she said agitatedly. 'You should have told me. I can't see him again.'

Grabbing her arm, Greg pulled her back. 'Sure you can. Look, you've got to face . . .'

'No!' Carina hit out at him, trying to break free. 'I can't. I won't!'

But Greg caught her other wrist. 'Listen to me. Carina, will you *listen* to me?' He shook her, and the shock of it made her stop struggling and stare at him. 'That's better. Now listen. Sometime or other you've got to face up to the truth. Luis Riveiro is wrong for you and always has been. Whatever sort of chemistry you had going for you, it couldn't surmount the fundamental differences between you. You tried once and it didn't work. And when you were willing to try again he couldn't even trust you enough to stay around and listen to an explanation. Isn't that true?'

'Yes, I suppose so,' Carina admitted reluctantly. 'But you don't . . .'

Greg held up a hand to stop her. 'Please, let me finish.' He looked into her worried, unhappy eyes and his voice softened. 'It's over, Carina. You've got to face up to it,' he said persuasively. 'And you've got pride. You didn't go running back to England—and you're not going to run away from this. You're going to go into that meeting with me and you're going to show Riveiro and the rest of them that you don't give a damn. To hell with him, Carina! You don't need him.'

Yes, I do, Carina's heart protested. My God, how I need him. But Greg was right in that she had pride, it made her stop panicking now, although her heart was still thumping painfully. She shook her head vehemently. 'Seeing him again isn't going to do me any good. I already *know* it's all over. And besides—all the people who are going to be at the meeting will know that I'm Luis's wife. It would be humiliating for him if I went to it with you.'

'And didn't he humiliate you when he accused you of being unfaithful?' Greg countered.

'That, too, was irrefutable. And now, after a couple of days had gone by and Carina had got over the first shock of despair, she was just beginning to feel angry at the injustice Luis had done her. But she said, 'I don't want revenge.'

'Good. Because hatred only dries up the heart. But you've got to put him out of your mind, put this whole episode right behind you and start again. And one way to start doing that is by going to the meeting and showing him that you don't care.' He paused and looked at her earnestly. 'Will you do that, Carina?' She hesitated before she answered, and seemed as if she was about to shake her head again, but Greg added, 'I'd ask you to do it for me, but I don't think you care enough for me to do that.'

Lifting her eyes, Carina looked into his face. He had been very kind to her in his efforts to atone for what he had done, and had kept his word, not making any attempt at a pass, even though he was attracted to her. And it was hardly his fault that Luis had taken everything the wrong way. Carina sighed and sat back in the seat. 'All right, I'll go. For you. But promise me that you won't—start a scene or anything. If that happens I shall just walk out.'

'Don't worry,' Greg assured her. Then he grinned. 'But if it does, I'll be right behind you. Riveiro's bigger than me.'

The implication that Greg was a coward was so manifestly false that Carina smiled, as she was meant to, but by the time the taxi drew up outside the building where the meeting was to take place her body had started to tremble in dreaded anticipation.

Taking her arm, Greg led her into the building and up

the stairs, but he let her go when they entered the meeting-room.

There were several people already there, mostly men, with just one other woman there, who was sitting at a small desk in the corner, presumably to take down the minutes of the meeting. Luis, too, was there. He was standing with his back to the door, talking to another man, and Carina, with sudden hypersensitivity, knew that he had deliberately placed himself like that so that he didn't have to look directly at Greg when he came in. Believing, as he did, that Greg was her lover, this must be quite a traumatic meeting for him, too, she realised.

Someone came forward to meet Greg, giving Carina a rather startled look as he did so, but hiding his surprise beneath a civil greeting. Greg stood chatting to him for a few minutes, and Carina saw the man that Luis was talking to glance up and see her. He gave Luis a nudge and the latter too, looked round, his shoulders braced. He saw Greg first and his jaw hardened perceptibly. Then he saw Carina. His face whitened and that look of murderous rage darkened his eyes. For a moment that seemed to stretch into eternity, they gazed at each other across the room, the air filled now not with the electricity of desire, but the tension of anger and outrage.

People began to look round at them, but the leading Portuguese partner quickly called to everyone to sit down. An extra chair was put at the table for Carina and she took her place next to Greg, her eyes fixed on the pad in front of her as she began to take notes. She didn't look at Luis again, but she was painfully aware of him, her heart beating so that she couldn't hear properly and only put down the odd sentence at random. Desperately, she tried to concentrate, but it was all she could do to stop her hand from shaking. In the end, she took the notepad off the table and held it in her lap so that no one could see that she was only writing nonsense.

Someone asked Luis a question, and they all waited for him to answer, but he didn't seem to have heard and they had to ask again. And once Greg used a rather technical phrase and she had to translate for him, the right words somehow coming into her mind. She felt Luis's eyes on her as she spoke, but she carefully looked away from him, her hands hot and slippery as she gripped her pen beneath the table.

At last the meeting was over. The senior partner stood up and said, 'Well, I think that is all, gentlemen. The necessary documents can now be drawn up and we can all meet to sign them, with our lawyers acting as witnesses, shall we say in two days? Very well, then at ten o'clock on Friday morning. Now *senhors*——' he bowed towards Carina '—and *senhora*, shall we take an aperitif before we go into lunch?'

She gave Greg a horrified look. 'You didn't tell me you were having lunch as well?'

'So what?' he said easily as he got to his feet. 'Why worry? You're doing fine.'

Everyone began to move around and talk, but Carina stayed close by Greg's side and tried to pretend she wasn't there, which was difficult when she was the only woman among so many men. The other woman secretary had gone out, presumably to get the aperitifs, and presently came back carrying a tray of drinks just as Greg excused himself to go to the cloakroom. Carina gave him a fiery glance, but he merely gave her a comically woeful look and left her alone.

'You speak Portuguese extremely well, *senhora*,' one of Greg's partners told her. She turned to speak to him, but had only been trying to make conversation for a few moments when Luis came over to her with two glasses in his hands.

'Your aperitif,' he said shortly, handing her one of the drinks.

'Thank you.' The words came out in a kind of croak, and she just prayed that Luis would go away. But he didn't. Instead, he just stood there until the other man got the message, and rather uncomfortably excused himself.

'You cruel little cat,' Luis grated at her as soon as he was out of earshot. 'Are you enjoying being here, rubbing salt into the wound?'

'I'm not. It wasn't my idea. I . . .'

'*His*, then,' Luis said scathingly, his eyes boring into her. 'But you let him bring you here to humiliate me.'

'No, I . . .' Her head came up. 'I don't have to take this from you.'

She went to step past him, but Luis's hand shot out and he grabbed her wrist. 'Just stay away in future.' His voice grew silky with threatened menace. 'If you come with him to the meeting on Friday, I won't be answerable for the consequences, do you understand?'

Carina stared at him, hardly recognising him as the same man who had told her that he loved and wanted her, only a few short days ago. His mouth was twisted with bitterness and scarcely controlled anger, his eyes bleak and fired only by hatred. She opened her mouth but couldn't speak, and after a moment he gave a curt nod and moved away.

When Greg returned a couple of minutes later, he

found her standing alone, apparently lost in thought, but actually staring down at the red marks on her wrist where Luis had gripped her so tightly.

At lunch, Carina sat as far away from Luis as possible, she and Greg leaving as soon as it was over.

'Let's walk,' Greg said as they came out on to the street. 'I'm playing in a charity match tomorrow and I need the exercise.' He glanced at her several times as she strode silently along beside him and, after a while, he said, 'Are you OK? Did Riveiro speak to you?'

'You mean my husband, don't you? He's that still, Greg.'

'All right, your husband. Did he say anything to you?'

'Yes. He warned me not to go to the meeting with you on Friday or he wouldn't be answerable for what might happen.'

'And what did you say?' Greg asked after giving a grunt of indignation.

'Nothing. I—I couldn't.'

'You should have stood up to him, Carina. You don't owe him anything.'

She was silent, pondering over that, but then realised that questions of debt didn't come into it, only feelings.

They walked on, and presently Greg said, 'Will you come and help me with this demonstration match tomorrow?'

Carina gave him a startled glance. 'You want me to caddie for you?'

Throwing back his head, Greg laughed in rich amusement. 'No, idiot! To translate.' He slipped his arm through hers. 'Afterwards, there will be a formal dinner at the club that we're invited to. Then, on Friday, I'd like to leave for the Algarve immediately after the meeting to sign the contracts.'

'You're not expecting me to go to that, are you?'

'Of course.'

'But I told you,' she began agitatedly. 'Luis threatened to . . .'

'To do what?' Greg interrupted. 'Think about it, Carina. They were just threats. There's no way he's going to make a scene in front of his business colleagues, especially when one of them is his client.' He paused and turned to face her. 'You're not afraid of him, are you?'

'Yes,' Carina admitted honestly but reluctantly. 'Yes, I'm afraid of him.'

'He can't hurt you—not when I'm around.'

'Oh, Greg, he already *has*! And going to that meeting today made him think that I was twisting the knife, being cruel. So now he'll do the same, if he can.'

'He can hardly love you, then, if he wants to hurt you,' Greg commented.

But he was wrong, Carina did at least know that. Where emotions were very deep, then so was the need to hit back when you were hurt. 'It will be much better if I don't go on Friday.'

'But I need you there,' Greg insisted. She didn't answer, and he took her hand and began to walk along again. 'Come on, let's find the famous monument to the old explorers that I've heard so much about.'

They found the white stone monument that stood right on the edge of the River Tagus, where fourteenth and fifteenth-century explorers had set out to discover the new world. It made a dazzling landmark from both land and sea, and gave a breathtaking view of the river when they took the lift to the top. The rest of the afternoon they spent exploring that area of the city, eating at a restaurant built on a pier extending into the river.

The next day, Carina had her first real opportunity to see just how famous Greg was. The golf course where he was going to play was a few miles from Lisbon, and literally hundreds of people had turned out to watch. It seemed that the event had been widely advertised by Greg's business partners, as it was good publicity for the holiday village, and several of them had come along in person. Greg was almost mobbed as soon as they arrived, early in the morning, and he had to shake hands with a great many people who were sponsoring the event, which was in aid of local charities. There was champagne and the usual Portuguese wines available, but Greg would only have coffee, and soon went out to practise before the actual match began.

'I haven't played for over two weeks,' he reminded Carina. 'I'm out of practice and I don't want to mess this up and disappoint people.'

He practised solidly for three hours, driving, putting, chip shots, the whole range, while Carina sat on the grass and watched. Then they walked over the course together, Carina helping him to concentrate by stopping people from going up to ask for autographs.

The match began at three, Greg playing against the club's own pro, a Spaniard. The pro was given a handicap, but he was no real match for Greg, and in the end it turned into a demonstration of just how well to play the course, his opponent often gallantly applauding his best shots. After the match there was a reception in the club house, at which there were masses of people, and then a dinner for what seemed only a few less. There were lots of photographers there, too, and when she tried to move away Greg put a firm hand on her arm and held her at his side.

It had been a long, hot, sunny day and Carina had had quite a few drinks in the course of it. Also, being in Greg's reflected limelight like this for the first time had been quite a strain—she felt as if her mouth was stretched into a permanent social smile. When at last they got in the car to drive back to Lisbon, Carina collapsed in her seat. 'God, I'm exhausted! Heaven knows how you must feel, playing in all that heat.'

Greg shrugged. 'I'm used to it. It's pleasant to be in the sun. When I play in Scotland, it always seems to rain. I'm never that lucky in Scotland.'

She laughed. 'Is it always like this? So many people, and so much handshaking and autographs?'

'No, this was just a friendly match, not serious at all. It's when you have one of the big open tournaments that things really get tense. You keep away from the crowds, then, as much as you can.'

He went on to talk about the way he travelled round the world, of matches he'd won and lost, of his business interests. It seemed a very nomadic life-style and prompted Carina to say, 'But where do you actually live? Do you have a permanent home?'

'Two,' Greg replied. 'I have an apartment in California, and a country cottage in the south of England. You know, with a thatched roof and roses round the door. But I don't get to stay at either of them for very long.' His voice lowered reflectively. 'Sometimes I don't even bother to go to them when I can.'

Carina looked at him in some astonishment. 'Why ever not?'

He gave one of his lazy shrugs. 'Because it's easier to

stay in hotels.' He paused, then added, 'And because there's no one to share them with.'

'I'm surprised you don't have a girl waiting in each continent,' she said flippantly.

Greg laughed, but said on a slightly wistful note, 'Just one will do.'

Her feminine curiosity overcoming caution, Carina said, 'Haven't you ever been married—or anything?'

His voice amused, Greg answered, 'I haven't ever been married, but I did have a pretty strong "or anything" once.' He paused, and when she didn't speak he said, 'Aren't you going to ask me what happened?'

'Do you want to tell me?'

'I was hoping you'd be interested enough to want to find out.'

'OK, so tell me,' Carina said, to please him.

Maybe Greg realised that she wasn't really interested in the way he wanted, but he said, 'I met a girl in England and we fell for each other. I leased a flat in London and she moved in with me, but I'd just begun to be really successful and to start travelling a lot. Also, I had to put in long hours of practice to get me up into the top professional bracket. So many players get to be quite good and win a few good tournaments, then fade away again. I was determined not to do that, so I took on all the work I could get.' He paused as they reached the toll booths at the beginning of the *autostrada* and he paid the fee.

'She couldn't take it,' he said as they drove on. 'She wanted a home and a nine-to-five man. Oh, she came with me for a year or so, but couldn't stand being left alone so much while I was practising and playing. She started staying behind while I went away to matches, and one day I came home to find that she'd gone.'

'Didn't you try to make it up?' Carina asked, remembering how she'd left Luis.

'No. She'd met someone else. I believe she's married to a bank clerk now and has a brood of kids.'

'It doesn't sound your style.'

'Oh, I don't know. It wasn't then, but it could be now; the kids, anyway. I've made enough money to pick and choose which tournaments I play in, and I've enough business interests, outside actually playing, for me to live on, if I wanted to. Not that I want to give up, of course, but I'd like to get married and have a family. In fact, I'm thinking of doing just that—any time now.'

'Really? Does the girl know?' Carina asked drily.

'She does now. No, don't say anything,' Greg said, as she opened her mouth to make an amazed protest. 'Just bear it in mind when you get round to going over your options.'

They fell into silence then, until they reached their hotel and went up together in the lift. At her door, Greg took her key from her and unlocked the door, pushing it open a little before he gave her back the key. He looked down at her, his grey eyes intent. 'I could think of a wonderful way to round off the day,' he said in soft suggestion.

Carina gave a small smile. 'You said no strings.'

He held up his hands, palms towards her. 'I meant it. This is definitely a ladies' invitation.'

She looked at the ground for a moment, then said, 'Sorry, but I think I'm going to prefer to be a wallflower for quite some time.'

'OK.' Putting a finger under her chin, he looked into her face for a moment then bent to kiss her, lingeringly.

'See you tomorrow.'

Going into her room, Carina undressed and showered, but sat on top of the bed, listening to the hum of the air-conditioning for a long time before she finally put out the light and went to sleep.

The next day was Friday, the day of Greg's final meeting to sign all the contracts, and the day they were to leave Lisbon for the Algarve. When Carina awoke, she had to decide whether she was going to obey Luis's demands and not go to the meeting, or whether to obey Greg and go. But rebellion set in almost immediately— why, for heaven's sake, had she to obey either of them? She would do what she damn well wanted. And, when it came down to it, Greg's wishes didn't really count at all. She would go to the meeting, yes, but not because of Greg. She would go, simply because she wasn't about to let Luis dictate to her. Not when she was innocent of all the things he'd charged her with.

So Greg was agreeably surprised to find her ready to accompany him, dressed in a crisp navy two-piece with a sailor collar, her hair taken up into her number two, business-executive style. Her face was pale, but there was a determined thrust to Carina's chin, and she was ready to face whatever Luis was about to throw at her. But the meeting, of course, was a complete anticlimax. Beyond giving her one look of utter fury, Luis completely ignored her. She checked through the translation of the documents once more for Greg, and then all the partners signed, afterwards shaking hands and drinking a toast to the success of their venture. And that was it. Luis left immediately the documents were signed, not staying for the toast, and she and Greg left soon afterwards to drive down to the Algarve.

After two days and nights of tension, Carina could hardly believe that it was over, and she found it difficult to unwind, but once they reached the Algarve Greg immediately plunged into work and she was kept very busy.

A suite had been booked for Greg in a hotel in the nearest town to the development site, and he was able to book a room for her on the same floor, so that she was always on hand when he needed her to answer calls and take dictation. Beneath his lazy exterior, Carina found that he was a glutton for work and took on a punishing schedule, often getting up at five in the morning to go out to the nearest golf course and practise while it was cool, then spending the morning supervising the construction of the development golf course, and in the afternoon playing in a tournament somewhere.

Carina found that she enjoyed the work, especially as Greg, realising how capable and efficient she was, gave her more and more to do, often leaving her to make quite important decisions. And she liked, too, to be busy, because then it took her mind off Luis and all the regrets that went with it. Mostly, now, she wished that she had never seen him again, never had that brief promise of happiness that had been so rudely torn from her.

In the evening, Greg liked to relax completely, and they would often drive to a restaurant and have a leisurely meal, Carina introducing him to the local dishes of chicken *piripiri*, a dish of chicken cooked in a spicy coating, or *cataplana*, which was a fish and shellfish stew. If he hadn't got to get up early to practise the next morning, they would sometimes go to a disco and dance to the early hours. Greg kept his promise not to make a pass, but he was male enough to take full advantage of holding her close when they danced, and he always kissed her goodnight, the kisses becoming deeper as the days passed. The kisses were pleasant enough, and it was nice to know that someone like Greg found her very attractive. But they weren't Luis's kisses; they didn't set her blood on fire or turn her legs to jelly.

Although Carina was putting off the decision, she knew that sometime soon she would have to make her mind up about Greg. Did she want to marry him and have his children? Better, surely, to have him and his family than none at all. Or would she look at them and always in her heart regret that they weren't Luis's children? Of only one thing was Carina absolutely sure: until she was divorced from Luis, she wouldn't go to bed with Greg—even if she did decide to marry him.

They had been on the Algarve, and the project developing well, for nearly a month, when Greg had to go to Lisbon again to the first regular monthly meeting of his partnership. Carina offered to stay behind to keep an eye on things, as it would be only a short visit, but Greg decided he wanted her with him, guessing— rightly—that she didn't want to take the risk of bumping into Luis, even though Greg assured her that he wouldn't be at the meeting.

The main tourist season was over now, and the hotels not so crowded, so they were able to get adjoining rooms in the hotel Greg had stayed at before. They had travelled up the previous evening so that he would be fresh for the meeting, a meeting that got quite heated once or twice, the partners taking to task a sub-contractor who was supposed to be building a marina for the holiday village and who was way behind schedule.

There were lots of other things to discuss and Carina was kept busy, finding that she could now translate almost simultaneously, which was an advantage for everyone, as they didn't have to keep stopping to translate for Greg. His partners now seemed to accept her as part of Greg's team and she felt little or no embarrassment at being with him this time. They seemed to realise that her being there, and on the development site, was helping things along, so even if they didn't approve they went along with it.

After lunch, Senhor Alvor, the partner who had given the party for Greg on his first day in Portugal, took him aside, and it wasn't until after they left that Greg told Carina what he'd said.

'It seems there's a stag party tonight at their local businessmen's club. They've invited me along.'

'A stag party?' Carina raised her eyebrows. 'Does that mean what I think it does?'

'Never having been to one in Portugal, I wouldn't know. But they said it was in aid of charity, and that I'd meet some useful business contacts there.'

'So you'll go, of course.'

'I don't want to leave you alone.'

'Greg, I'm not a child! I can take care of myself for one evening. I'll look in the paper to see what's on, and perhaps take myself to a film.'

'Are you sure you don't mind?'

'No, of course not. After all, we're not tied to each other in any way.'

'But I'd like to be,' Greg said earnestly. 'Carina, I . . .'

'No, please.' She looked at him pleadingly. 'Not yet, Greg.'

'All right.' He turned away, his mouth grim. 'But it's

getting harder every day, Carina.'

At seven, he knocked on the communicating door between their rooms and called out that he was leaving. Carina shouted goodbye and finished changing for the concert performance that she'd decided to go to, putting on a pair of black silk evening trousers, a white silk blouse and a loose black sequinned jacket. Her hair was combed into her number three style and she was just adding long jet earrings when there was a knock at her door. She went quite unsuspectingly to open it—and stood frozen with shock when she saw that the unexpected caller was Luis!

CHAPTER EIGHT

FOR a few fantastic heartbeats, hope rose as she thought that he might have come to make it up, but then Carina saw the icy coldness in Luis's eyes and the hope died stillborn.

'May I come in?' he asked shortly when she didn't speak.

Slowly, she moved aside and closed the door behind him. 'What do you want?'

He turned and looked her over. 'Going out to see who else you can pick up, now that your boyfriend is out of the way for the evening?' he demanded harshly.

Her cheeks flushed, Carina went to the door and opened it. 'Get out! You heard me,' she went on when he didn't move. 'I don't have to take that from you. Get out of my room.'

Crossing to her, Luis pulled the door from her grasp and banged it shut. 'Not until I've said what I came to say.'

'You've said enough already.'

Carina headed for the bedside phone, but Luis grabbed her arm and swung her round to face him. For a moment they stared at one another, both blazingly angry—Luis, his jaw tight, and his fingers digging into her flesh.

'Why have you come here?' she demanded.

'To give you this.' Taking a large envelope from his jacket pocket, Luis held it out to her.

'What is it?'

'The official notice that I'm filing for a divorce.'

She looked into his face for a moment, then said, 'Let go of me.'

He did so, and she rubbed her arm before taking the envelope from him and opening it. She took out a legal-looking document and glanced at it briefly. 'All right, so you've given it to me. Now what?'

'Do you intend to defend the petition?'

'No, why should I? I offered you a divorce years ago.'

'In that case, I would like you to sign this other document to say that you won't be submitting any defence.' And he took a second paper from his pocket.

'What do you mean, defence?' Carina asked suspiciously. 'We've been apart for four years; can't we just have the marriage ended?'

'Not when the petition is adultery.'

Carina stared at him. 'What do you mean?'

'You know damn well what I mean! I'm petitioning for divorce on the grounds of adultery, and I'm citing Summers as the co-respondent.'

'But you can't do that!' Carina exclaimed in horror. 'It isn't true.'

Luis laughed scornfully. 'Not true? When you're practically sharing a room with him?' And he gestured towards the communicating door.

'That door is locked,' Carina declared hotly. 'Try it yourself, if you don't believe me.'

'It wouldn't make any difference,' Luis said harshly. 'I already have as much evidence as I need to get a ruling in my favour.'

Carina became very still, staring at him. 'No, you

haven't,' she said finally, 'because there isn't any to get.'

'No? Then what the hell do you call these?' In bitter triumph, he thrust a folder of photographs at her.

'What are they?'

'See for yourself.'

'No. I don't want to know.'

'Then I'll damn well *make* you look!' With a quick stride, he caught hold of her and held her arms behind her back, pulling her up against him. Then, with his free hand, he took the photos from the folder and held them up in front of her face, one by one, afterwards letting them fall on the bed. The photographs were all of her and Greg. There were several taken when they were dancing and Greg was holding her very close, a couple of them both at the hotel pool when they'd gone for a midnight swim one night and Greg was towelling her dry, one taken on the beach when she'd been sunbathing topless and Greg was leaning over her, his hand on her waist. The last was of them kissing goodnight in the hotel corridor, only what had been an innocent enough kiss looked as if Greg was hunched over her and was about to take her into the room. She didn't remember any of them being taken; people were always taking photos on holiday and she hadn't paid any attention when flashes went off nearby. And Greg was famous, she'd got used to people taking his photograph.

After the first couple, Carina had tried to turn away, but Luis jerked her head up, making her gasp. 'Look at them, you lying bitch! Look at them the way I had to.'

Tears gathered at the corners of her eyes, but Carina blinked them back, determined not to let him see how deeply his accusations were hurting her.

'So what do you think of them?' Luis said as he

dropped the last one on the bed. 'Edifying, aren't they?'

Turning her head to look at him over her shoulder, Carina said sadly, 'Oh Luis, what have you done?'

'I set an enquiry agent to follow you. I would have left you alone if you'd kept away from that second meeting. But I told you I'd make you pay for it. So when you dared to defy me, and turned up, hanging on his arm . . .'

With a sudden movement, Carina got one arm free and swung round to face him. 'For the last time, Luis, he isn't my lover, he's my boss. I'm working for him.'

Luis laughed derisively, pointing to the photographs. 'These are hardly the evidence of a platonic relationship. What was he going when he was holding you so close—giving you dictation?' he sneered.

'No—comfort.'

For a moment, Luis's brows drew into a frown, but then he dismissed the idea out of hand. 'You're wasting your time. There's no way you'll ever convince me that he isn't your lover. But if you want to fight me in court, then go ahead—we'll see whose word is believed.'

'Why are you doing this? You'll only be dragging your own name through the dirt. You can't possibly want that.'

Luis's grip on her arm tightened cruelly. 'You've already flaunted your lover in front of my business colleagues. By now, everyone in Lisbon knows about it, knows that you deliberately set out to humiliate me. So what the hell difference does it make to me? And this way your famous boyfriend will be shown up for what he is.'

'And that's what you really want, isn't it?' Carina demanded angrily. 'You just can't stand to think that I preferred another man to you. What's the matter, Luis? Does that deflate your ego? Does it make you feel unmanned when you think of me being made love to by someone else? Does it . . .'

'*Cerra a boca!*' Luis started to shake her, but Carina tried to break free. For a few moments they struggled wildly, but then Carina was brought up short by the bed and fell on to it, with Luis on top of her.

'Let me go! Damn you, let go of me!' Carina yelled at him, trying to scratch his face.

But Luis let his weight rest on her, making her breathless, and he caught her wrists, holding them above her head. Still Carina fought; goaded into fury, she arched her body, trying to throw Luis off, and sank her teeth into his wrist.

He jerked his arm away, and again she tried to claw him. They rolled on the bed among the scattered photographs, Carina beating at him for the few seconds she was on top, but then Luis heaved her off and came down on top of her, his hand in her hair.

'Get off me! God, how I hate you!' she shouted at him. But the next moment his mouth was on hers, silencing her, as he kissed her with a savagery that was full of hurt and rage.

Carina tried desperately to break free, twisting her head from side to side, but Luis's grip tightened, holding her prisoner beneath his mouth. She tried to bite him, and he cursed as he felt blood on his tongue, but still he went on kissing her, his rage turning to desire. And suddenly Carina was kissing him back, her mouth opening beneath his.

'*Mãe de Deus!*' His hands were on her clothes, tearing them in his haste. His mouth left hers as he kissed her eyes, her throat, his heated breath scorching her skin, setting her blood on fire.

Carina put her hands in his hair, clinging to him, trying to draw him down to return his kisses. 'Luis! Oh, Luis.'

His hand was on her breast, urgent in its raging need, shaking with desire, his breath a shuddering moan of hunger. He would have kissed her breast, but Carina forced his head up so that she could drown in his kisses, saying his name over and over against his mouth, low sounds of animal passion that nevertheless cried out her aching longing and frustration.

His fingers tightened in involuntary passion, making Carina cry out. Lifting his head, Luis looked down at her, his eyes glistening with raging torment, driven by a desperate desire of which he had entirely lost control.

Carina arched her body towards him, pulling at his clothes, trying to get near him, to touch him. He gave a great groan when she at last touched his skin. 'Oh, God! Oh, God!' Lifting himself on his elbow, Luis tugged at the fastening of her trousers, impatiently knocking one of the photos out of the way. In doing so, it turned over, and registered on his brain. He became very still, staring at it, then suddenly swore and stood up. 'You witch! Oh, God, you evil little temptress.' With trembling hands, he pushed his hair back off his forehead and did up his shirt, while Carina gazed unbelievingly up at him, too demoralised to speak.

'Nothing's changed,' Luis said savagely. 'Now I want that divorce more than ever. I want to be rid of you. I never want to see or hear of you again!'

After he had stormed out of the room, slamming the door behind him, Carina just lay there, staring up at the ceiling, too emotionally drained even to cry. It grew dark outside, but still she lay there, unmoving, until the air-conditioning made her feel cold. At last, she got up and switched on the light.

Her silk blouse had been torn apart, and her lace bra was also ruined where Luis's impatient hands had pulled it off. Her jacket wasn't so bad, but it didn't matter—Carina knew that she would never wear that outfit again. Her hair was loose and dishevelled, and her ear-rings she found on the bed among the photographs. Those damn photographs! Quickly, Carina picked them up, tore them into small pieces and flushed them down the loo. Not that it would make any difference, she knew; Luis could easily have more copies made, but at least she didn't have to look at them any more.

Stripping off her clothes, Carina slipped under the shower and soaped herself, trying to wash away the feel of Luis's hands on her skin. But that was impossible. Impossible, too, for the stinging spray to wash away his memory from her brain as she would like it to have done. It was just something else she was going to have to live with. But at least it helped her to realise that she must leave Portugal at once, that she should never have stayed.

Putting on her thick white bathrobe, Carina went into the bedroom and phoned the airport, booking a flight on the first available plane to England, which wasn't until the following evening, much later than she wanted. But, if necessary, she could always wait at the airport. Now that she had made up her mind, she couldn't wait to get away, so she also rang down to the desk and asked them to have her bill ready in the morning. It didn't take long to pack, she hadn't brought many things with her to

Lisbon, most of them had been left behind at their hotel on the Algarve, but she was quite willing to abandon those if Greg cut up rough.

Her packing done, there was nothing left to do except the one thing she'd been avoiding. Crossing to the table, Carina reluctantly picked up the divorce petition and the document that Luis had wanted her to sign. Carefully now, she read them through. The petition listed dates and places—the hotels in Lisbon and the Algarve— where Luis alleged that adultery had taken place. The other form was to say that she would submit no defence, an admission of guilt, in other words. Carina read them through once more, then deliberately picked up a pen and signed the second document. Now Luis would have what he wanted, and they would be free of each other at last. Free to hate each other, instead of secretly longing for a reconciliation.

It would have been easy to just write a letter to Greg and slip away the next morning, but Carina waited until he knocked on the communicating door.

'Hey, you ready for breakfast, Carina?'

'Yes, I'm ready.' She unlocked the door and opened it. 'Greg, I have to talk to you.'

His eyes narrowed as he took in the way she was dressed, and then he saw the case on the bed.

'You're leaving?'

'Yes.'

'What happened?'

'Nothing. I just realised that—that I'm wasting your time hanging around here, so . . .'

'I'll be the judge of that,' Greg interrupted shortly. 'I want you around, you know that.'

'Greg, I'm sorry, but I'm not in love with you and I

can't ever marry you. I wish I could,' she added, almost desperately. 'It would be wonderful to love you and be your wife. But I—I just can't.'

'It's Riveiro, isn't it? You're still in love with him?' She nodded and he said, 'What made you come to this sudden decision?'

'I realised that I wasn't being fair to you and . . .'

'Don't lie to me, Carina,' he said harshly, his brows drawing into a frown. 'I don't deserve that.'

She bit her lip. 'I'm sorry, I didn't want . . . He came here last night. Luis. He said he wanted a divorce. He's going to sue for one.'

'Well, isn't that what you want, too? Surely you don't want to stay tied to him?'

Shaking her head, Carina said, 'You don't understand. He wants to divorce me on the grounds of adultery with you.'

'But we haven't made love.'

'He won't believe that,' Carina explained tiredly. 'And he has photographs of us together that make it— look as if we have.'

Greg shrugged. 'All right, so let him. It doesn't make any difference to me how you get your freedom, so long as you're free.'

'I'm sorry,' she said again. 'But you've always known that I love Luis. I haven't pretended otherwise. And now I know that if I can't have him, then I don't want anyone else. It wouldn't work and it wouldn't be fair on either of us.' She braced her shoulders. 'So I'm leaving, Greg. Today. I've booked a flight back to England.'

'What about your job as my assistant?'

'There are plenty of people down on the Algarve who speak English. You'll find someone else.'

'Carina.' He strode towards her, bent on making her change her mind, but she quickly put up her hands to hold him off. 'Don't do this,' he said urgently. 'Stay with me. You might change your mind.'

But Carina shook her head. She reached up to kiss him, then said huskily, 'Goodbye, Greg. I'll never forget you.' And ran back into her room before he could stop her, closing the door and locking it behind her.

He didn't try to follow her or contact her. Carina half expected that he would, and waited for half an hour before she rang down to room service and asked them to send breakfast up to her. There were so many impatient hours to wait until her flight left. Carina ate slowly, and was still on her first cup of coffee when the phone rang. She almost left it unanswered, thinking it might be Greg, but eventually picked it up. '*Olá?*'

'*Senhora*, this is the reception desk. There is a driver here with a car for you. The driver asks if he may bring a message up to you.'

'Are—are you sure it's for me? I'm not expecting anyone.'

'Oh, yes, the man is quite certain.'

'Well, all right. I suppose you'd better let him come up.'

She waited, wondering if this was some ploy of Greg's to keep her here, and opened the door very cautiously when the knock came. But she recognised the man standing outside in chauffeur's uniform, and couldn't have been more surprised. 'José?'

'*Senhora.*' The man smiled at her warmly, and held out a letter. He was the general factotum at Luis's Lisbon house, acting as butler, handyman, chauffeur to Luis's mother, and he also did any other job that was required. He was married to the cook-cum-housekeeper, the two of them running the house very efficiently between them. They had always been friendly towards Carina while she lived there, so that she had often sneaked down to the kitchen to see them, even though Luis's mother had disapproved.

'José, how are you? How is Lucia?'

They talked for a few minutes, then he said, 'Please, *senhora*, read the letter. Senhora Riveiro wishes to see you.'

Carina's eyes widened in surprise, and she tore open the envelope, taking the letter over to the window to read. It was short, written in English with the shaky hand of someone who was old or ill. Not the curt note she'd expected, but an almost humble request for her to call. 'Please come,' the note finished. 'It is most important that I speak with you as soon as possible.'

Her first impulse was to ignore the note and throw it away, but the urgency of it made her hesitate. Senhora Riveiro had stressed that she wanted to see her at once. A great fear suddenly entered Carina's heart that Luis might have had an accident and been hurt. He had been so mad when he left her last night, and the Portuguese were notoriously bad drivers. Quickly, she turned. 'Has anything happened to Senhor Luis?'

José looked puzzled. 'Why, no, *senhora*.'

Her heart began to beat again and she reread the note, then thought that she had nothing to lose by going to see the older woman. She had time to kill, and she would always be curious if she didn't.

'Could you take me to the airport after I've seen Senhora Riveiro?'

'But certainly.'

And so, about half an hour later, Carina found herself stepping once more, and most unexpectedly, through the wide double doorway of the Riveiro house. It hadn't changed much; the furniture and décor were still the same, and it was still spotlessly clean and smelt of too much polish. Lucia opened the door to her and was obviously pleased to see her, but the maid soon led Carina upstairs to Senhora Riveiro's bedroom on the first floor. Lucia knocked, and when a voice answered she held the door open for Carina to go in.

Luis had told her that his mother had been ill, but even so Carina wasn't prepared for the vast change in the older woman. When Carina had left in defeat, Senhora Riveiro had been a tall, upright woman of sixty with hair only partly touched by grey, a woman who ruled her household and had great pride. Now she sat in a chair by the window, with a shawl round her shoulders, even though the day was warm. Her hair was completely grey and she seemed somehow diminished, in spirit as well as in size, her once strong hands lying in her lap, thin and withered. As she looked at her, Carina realised at once what Luis had not told her; that his mother's illness was terminal; she would never recover.

For a few moments neither woman spoke, both of them remembering their last bitter parting, but then Senhora Riveiro made a weak gesture towards a chair placed near her own. 'Thank you for coming. Please sit down.'

Carina did so, determined to remember what this woman had done to her, and not let it be lost under present pity.

'You look—unhappy,' Senhora Riveiro commented.

'Do I?' Carina answered shortly, wondering if her

mother-in-law merely wanted to gloat once more over a second triumph.

'I heard that you were in Portugal again.' The older woman lifted tired, almost tormented eyes to look at her. 'Luis didn't tell me, it was someone else. When you came—the change in Luis, it was like a miracle. He came alive again. Alive as he has not been since—since you left.'

'I think you mean, since you drove me away, don't you?' Carina said acidly, unable to resist.

To her amazement, Senhora Riveiro slowly nodded. 'Yes, that is so. I—I thought it was for the best. I thought that Luis would soon forget you and marry again. Give me grandchildren. But he always refused to get a divorce. And—and then I saw that he always hoped you would come back.' She paused to lift a lace handkerchief to her lips with a shaking hand. 'And when you did come he was so full of hope and determination. He didn't tell me you were here—but I knew. When he left for the villa, I knew that you were there and he was going to ask you to come back to him.'

Carina looked at her for a moment, and then down at her own hands, tightly held together in her lap.

'But you refused, did you not? I have never seen my son so unhappy. It is even worse for him now than the first time.'

She paused, but Carina said nothing. What was there to say? She certainly had no intention of relating the whole story to this woman who had been her enemy.

'Carina, please, I must know: is it because of me that you refused to return to him? Because, if it is, I assure you that you have nothing to fear from me. I will leave this house and go into a nursing home. You will not have to live with me or see me—ever.' Her voice broke and she coughed a little, but then went on speaking as Carina stared at her with startled eyes. 'I ruined my son's life, I know that now, and I don't wish to be the cause of ruining it again. Please, go back to him. Make him happy. He loves you. I have an illness. I—I do not think I have . . .'

Carina put out a hand, gesturing her to silence. 'Please. Don't torture yourself. It wasn't because of you. It was—something else that came between us. A—a misunderstanding.'

Senhora Riveiro looked at her sad face for a long moment, then said, 'Forgive me, but are you still in love with Luis?' And when Carina nodded silently, she continued, 'And I know that he is very much in love with you. So surely this—misunderstanding—can be resolved? If you go to him . . .'

Carina's head came up. 'That wouldn't work,' she answered shortly.

'Wouldn't it? Or is it just pride that is holding you back? Are you both going to be unhappy for the rest of your lives because of it?'

A spark of determination, that Carina recognised, had come to the older woman's eyes. Only this time it was on her side, not against her. 'You really mean it,' she said wonderingly. 'You really want us to get back together.' She shook her head. 'It's too late. I'm leaving today and going back to England.'

'Carina.' The older woman seemed to muster all her resources as she leaned forward. 'You say that you love my son. Won't you then, for *his* sake, make one last attempt to make up your differences with him? I don't want him to be alone for the rest of his life, alone and bitter. *Please* do this for him.'

Getting to her feet, Carina said, 'Why don't you ask *him*?'

'Because he isn't here. He left last night for his house in the mountains. The place he goes to when life here becomes unbearable. Where he shuts himself away and licks his wounds. The wounds I gave him,' his mother admitted, the lustre leaving her eyes again.

Crossing to the window, Carina stared blindly out at the street below as she tried to think. Was there a remote chance for them? Even now? Luis's mother didn't know everything, of course, not about last night or Luis's belief that she and Greg were lovers. But she seemed so sure that Luis still loved her. And he had said so himself, until that terrible moment when he had found Greg in her room. Could she convince him of the truth? Or would it just degenerate into another terrible scene like last night? Carina shuddered, remembering. But she remembered so many other things, too. At last she turned and said, 'All right. I'll have one last try. Exactly where is his house?'

'*Thank you.*' The older woman's voice was deep with gratitude. 'It is in the mountains near Monchique. It is called Casa de Aguias, the house of eagles. José will take you there.'

'No, I'd rather go alone. But I'll borrow your car, if I may.'

'Of course. When will you go?'

Carina shrugged. 'If I'm going at all, it may as well be now.'

Monchique was back in the Algarve, a small town by Portuguese standards, in a range of mountains to the west of the area, and to reach it Carina had to travel most of the way on the same road out of Lisbon. But then she turned off and gradually began to climb, reaching the town a couple of hours later. Here she stopped to buy petrol and to consult the map that José had drawn for her. Luis's house was further on, even higher up in the mountains, and she had to thread her way through the town, go round a roundabout and up a very steep and narrow cobbled street, just praying that nothing was coming the other way.

After Monchique, the landscape changed completely, and Carina drove through woods of pine trees, their scent reaching her through the open windows of the car in the clean air. At intervals she would pass a *mirador*, where there were beautiful views over the rolling valleys below, the lower hills the shape of giant anthills. She was very high now, almost three thousand feet, and the woods had thinned out considerably, so that she could see the red sandstone with here and there an outcrop of granite rocks. She began to look out for the turning to Luis's house, afraid of missing it, but found it quite easily and turned down the much narrower road. After only a short way Carina saw the house sign, Casa de Aguias, and turned into the driveway.

She drove up towards the house, then turned into the woods, the pine branches cracking under the tyres, and parked the car beneath the shelter of some trees. She began to walk towards the house, but then remembered something, and went back to fiddle with the engine and hide the part she'd taken off under a stone. Luis wasn't the only one who could sabotage a car!

It was a beautiful house, almost a log cabin, that blended in perfectly with its surroundings, long and low with a stone chimney. Luis's car was parked at the side of the house, near a stable, the doors of which were standing open. Was he out riding? Carina walked up the stone steps to the front door and knocked, but there was no answer. Gingerly, she tried the handle and found that the door was unlocked. After a moment's hesitation, she went inside.

'Luis?' He didn't answer her call, so she was free to look around; at the living-room, with its stone fireplace and big comfortable settee, at the small but compact kitchen, and the one bedroom with a bathroom opening off it. The bedroom was dominated by a big double bed, but then Luis needed a big one to accommodate his long frame. There were pictures on the walls, books, a music centre in the living-room. Yes, this was his retreat now, as the villa could no longer be because of his memories of her. And if this attempt failed, would this place no longer be a haven for him, either? For a few seconds, Carina was tempted to run away, to leave him what little he had left. But no, that would be a cowardly thing to do, and she was determined now to make this one last try for happiness, a resolve that was encouraged when she saw a photograph of herself on one of the bedside cabinets, a photograph that Luis had taken himself on their honeymoon, when she was laughing at the camera, the wind in her hair and love in her eyes.

Picking it up, she carried the photo into the living-room and was looking down at it a few minutes later when Luis strode into the room.

'José? I heard the car. Has anything happened to . . .' He stopped in stunned astonishment when he saw her. 'You!'

'H-hello, Luis.' Her fingers tightened nervously on the photograph, gaining strength from it.

'What the hell are you doing here? How did you find this place?' he rasped, his face darkening with anger.

'José told me how to find it.'

'Did he, indeed?' Luis said in a tone that boded ill for his old servant.

'Yes, I—I told him I wanted to see you urgently.'

'Why? I've already told you that I never want to see you again.'

'I know. But you left my room in such a hurry last night that you left something behind.' Putting down the photograph, Carina opened her bag and took out the two documents. 'The divorce petition and the document you wanted me to sign.'

'Why have you brought them here? You could have sent them to my office.'

'I was going to,' Carina admitted. 'But—something happened to make me change my mind.'

'And did you sign it?' Luis asked sneeringly, fully expecting her to say no.

'Yes. Yes, I signed it.'

He stared at her, his body suddenly tense. 'So you admit your guilt? Admit that you and Summers were lovers?'

She shook her head. 'No, I signed it because I was just sick of the whole thing. I wanted it to be over and done with. I just—just didn't care anymore.' Lifting her head, Carina looked him fully in the face. 'But now something has happened to make me—change my mind.' And she deliberately tore through both the papers. 'If you want a divorce on the grounds of adultery, Luis, then you're going to have to fight me for it. Because I've never been unfaithful to you—not with my body or in my heart.'

'You have! I found Summers in your room. And I found out he told the manager of the hotel he was your husband.'

'Only because he couldn't find anywhere else to stay. Greg tried to contact me from Lisbon and got worried when the hotel told him they hadn't seen me for two days, when you persuaded me to stay at the villa. They told him I hadn't come back the previous night, so he went to the Algarve to try to find me. He waited until late, and couldn't find anywhere to stay and there were no spare rooms in the hotel, so . . .' Carina shrugged. '. . . he said he was my husband just so that he could get a bed for the night.'

'And you expect me to believe that?' Luis sneered. 'When you've been with him ever since?'

'But it was you who drove me into getting a lift from him back to Lisbon,' Carina pointed out. 'You left me stranded.'

Luis gave a harsh laugh. 'And was it I who made you stay with him, work for him?'

For a moment Carina was silent, but then said, 'Yes, in a way, I think it was. Because in my heart I think I always hoped that you would realise you were wrong, and come for me.'

Luis stiffened and she saw his hands ball into tight fists. Turning, he strode towards the doorway and her heart plummeted as Carina thought that he was going to walk away, but in the doorway he paused, his back to her. 'You said that something had happened to make you change your mind—what was it?'

She was silent for a moment, wondering to tell him about his mother, but decided not to yet. So she said, 'You asked me why I'd brought those papers instead of sending them to your office; but you brought them to my hotel yourself last night instead of sending them. If you'd really hated me, you would have done anything rather than see me again. I think you still care about me, Luis, however angry you feel. I—I realised that. And so I came.'

'You're mistaken,' Luis said curtly. 'I feel nothing for you.'

'Really?' Carina pointed to the photograph in its silver frame. 'Then why do you keep this by your bed?'

He turned and his jaw tightened. 'That isn't you; that's the girl I married. You and she are no longer the same woman.'

'Oh, but we are. More than you'll ever know.' She took a step towards him and lifted a hand in a pleading gesture, but Luis swung round again and put a hand on either side of the door, his knuckles showing white. Carina bit her lip, wondering how on earth she was to melt this barrier of ice he had built round himself. After a moment, she said, 'You know, I think our mistake— no, our misfortune—was to fall so head over heels in love when we first met and get married so quickly. We didn't have time to *be* in love, to gradually build a wall of love around ourselves by being loving towards each other. I know we had sex, and that was a wonderful part of it, but we were always so rushed and there were—other people around.' Carina paused, then went on, 'I think that love is something you have to make grow, to build up over the years. But we weren't given—didn't have a chance to . . .' Her voice broke and she turned away blinking hard.

When, at length, she looked at Luis again, Carina expected to see him still with his back to her, but he had turned to face her. There was something different about him; the tension was still there, but it was different now, not angry, but an electric, physical tautness. Carina caught her breath, a sudden hope rising in her heart.

Taking a step towards her, Luis said harshly, 'Do you swear that you and Summers were never lovers?'

'Yes,' she answered clearly. 'And I swear that there has never been anyone else but you.'

He stared at her, the bleakness gone from his eyes, then slowly opened his arms. 'Then—come.'

But Carina shook her head. 'No. First you have to swear that you believe me. Because if you've any doubts, it won't work. Much as I love you, Luis, I . . .'

Her words were lost as Luis strode forward and took her in his arms. 'It will work,' he said forcefully. 'I'll make it work. And I do believe you, *cara*, but I was so torn by jealousy that I think I went mad! To be so close to happiness . . .'

'Oh, I know. I know.' Carina clung to him tightly. 'Don't ever let anything part us again. I couldn't bear it.'

'Nothing will. I swear it. Oh, *meu amor*.' Taking her head between his hands, Luis kissed her fiercely, trying with all his love and need for her to drown out the mistakes of the past.

Carina returned his embrace as ardently as she knew how, but when he lifted his head, his breath ragged, she gazed into his face with frightened eyes. 'Luis, I'm so afraid.'

'Don't be. I'll take care of you.' His arms went round her, holding her close, letting her feel his strength. 'We'll be all right this time. We'll build that wall of love around us, until it's so thick and solid it will be impossible for it to fall or break. And you don't have to worry about my mother; we'll find somewhere to live and ...'

Carina smiled and shook her head. 'No, I don't think so. You know I told you something had happened to bring me here? It was your mother. She told me where to find you—and she also told me that you were still in love with me. So I hardly think it would be fair to leave her on her own after she's brought us back together, do you?'

Luis was gazing at her in astonishment. 'My mother told you? But how?' Carina went to answer, but his arms tightened. 'No, not now. Tell me later. Right now, I have something far more important on my mind.' He kissed her hungrily, and soon passion engulfed them, the raging need of desire searing through their veins. Somehow, Carina found herself lying on the big fur hearthrug on the floor, their clothes scattered around them, but then Luis swung her up in his arms and carried her into the bedroom, kissing her as he held her.

He made love with all the pent-up hunger of the lost years, and it was only when they were lying exhausted in each other's arms that they again found the time for words. They talked of their future, of their shared wish to start a family as soon as possible.

'I'm sure your mother would like a grandchild,' Carina said dreamily. 'Even if it does have fair hair.'

Luis raised himself on one elbow and smiled, as he gently stroked her hair from her damp forehead. 'A girl just like you.'

'No, a boy just like you,' she smiled back.

Luis laughed, and to see him laugh so happily was so wonderful that tears came to Carina's eyes.

'*Cara*, what is it? ' He was immediately all concern.

'Nothing, I'm just so happy, that's all.'

He kissed away her tears and began to caress her, the light of desire again growing in his eyes. But he was gentle now, his first savage hunger more than appeased. 'How about starting that family now?' he said suggestively.

Carina chuckled. 'I thought we already had.' She put her arms around his neck. 'But I'm quite willing to try again.' She began to kiss him, but suddenly raised her head. 'Oh! I've just thought of something. *My* mother isn't going to like this.'

To which, of course, there was only one reply.

Harlequin Temptation dares to be different!

Once in a while, we Temptation editors spot a romance that's truly innovative. To make sure *you* don't miss any one of these outstanding selections, we'll mark them for you.

EDITOR'S CHOICE

When the "Editors' Choice" fold-back appears on a Temptation cover, you'll know we've found that extra-special page-turner!

THE

Temptation

EDITORS

Spot-1B

Harlequin American Romance

Romances that go one step farther...
American Romance

Realistic stories involving people you can relate to and care about.

Compelling relationships between the mature men and women of today's world.

Romances that capture the core of genuine emotions between a man and a woman.

Join us each month for four new titles wherever paperback books are sold.
Enter the world of American Romance.

Amro-1

Harlequin Presents

Coming Next Month

Available in February wherever paperback books are sold, or through
Harlequin Reader Service:

In the U.S.
901 Fuhrmann Blvd.
P.O. Box 1397
Buffalo, N.Y. 14240-1397

In Canada
P.O. Box 603
Fort Erie, Ontario
L2A 5X3

ATTRACTIVE, SPACE SAVING BOOK RACK

Display your most prized novels on this handsome and sturdy book rack. The hand-rubbed walnut finish will blend into your library decor with quiet elegance, providing a practical organizer for your favorite hard-or soft-covered books.

Only $9.95

Approximately 16" x 8" when assembled

Assembles in seconds!

To order, rush your name, address and zip code, along with a check or money order for $10.70* ($9.95 plus 75¢ postage and handling) payable to *Harlequin Reader Service*:

Harlequin Reader Service
Book Rack Offer
901 Fuhrmann Blvd.
P.O. Box 1396
Buffalo, NY 14269-1396

Offer not available in Canada.

*New York and Iowa residents add appropriate sales tax.

BKR-1A

Keepsake

 Harlequin Books

You're never too young to enjoy romance. Harlequin for you . . . and Keepsake, young-adult romances destined to win hearts, for your daughter.

Pick one up today and start your daughter on her journey into the wonderful world of romance.

Two new titles to choose from each month.